Tied by Blood

Emily Davidson

DEDICATION

This fist novel is dedicated to all aspiring novelists out there.
Don't give up, you'll make it.

ACKNOWLEDGMENTS

To everyone who encouraged me, thank you. You know who you are and I honestly could not have done this without you. Thanks is also due to Mary Fahrer for her incredible cover design.

CHAPTER 1

Jake Henderson knelt in the snow, a bouquet of flowers in his
hand. He stared at the dates on the tombstone: *how can it have
been ten years already?* But it had been; ten years to the day since
his wife had passed away. No—that made it sound far too
peaceful. And it had been anything but.

Sighing, Jake went to place the flowers on the grave. It was
only then that he noticed there was another bunch of flowers
already there. Judging by the fact that there was only a very light
dusting of snow on top of them, whoever put them there must
have come less than an hour ago.

Too bad, Jake thought as he placed his flowers on top of the
other bouquet. *I could have used some company.* He kissed his fingers
then placed them over Margie's name. Then he got up, brushed
the snow from his jeans and headed back to his car.

Who had left those flowers? Jake supposed it was possible
that it had just been a passing stranger who wanted to do a good
deed. But the far more likely possibility was that it had been one
of his children who had put them there. After all, neither he nor

Margie had any family still living in this area, and their few friends had moved on. Thinking of his kids sent a jolt of pain and anger rippling up through Jake's body to join the grief he was feeling. *They couldn't have called first to see if maybe their father wanted to join them at the cemetery? Or do they just not care anymore?*

He knew the answer to that.

But a cemetery was no place to be having these thoughts. It wasn't as if thinking harsh thoughts about the living would bring the dead back to life. Although, now he came to think of it, Jake was forced to admit that he didn't know whether or not his children were even alive. Jake started his car and drove out of the graveyard. Only when he was on the road heading home did he resume his train of thought.

He hadn't spoken to either of his children since they had moved out of his house a year and a half apart. Occasionally he felt a twinge of guilt about that but then he remembered that neither of them had bothered to pick up the phone and call him either.

Margie had been the glue that held them all together; with her gone, everyone spread in their own direction, dealt with the grief in their own way. But Jake had been the worst. His way of dealing with the pain had been to use alcohol; when that didn't cut it any more, he had turned to drugs. To say he had been a terrible father would be putting it mildly. Not that he'd ever raised a hand to either of his children; he had rarely even raised his voice. But he hadn't done much else for them either.

Jake slammed on his brakes, the flashing lights ahead of him shaking his thoughts back into the present. He was looking at the back parking lot of a flower shop, lit up under harsh fluorescent lights. An ambulance and multiple police cars added their colors to the mix. The whole area was roped off with bright yellow crime scene tape, and there were several people standing out in the snow.

Some stood in little groups talking amongst themselves, clutching Styrofoam cups of steaming coffee and stamping their feet to keep warm. Others walked about with large cameras around their necks, snapping pictures of anything and everything. Still others stood in a cluster near the back door, looking at something on the ground. Jake couldn't make out exactly what it was, and that was probably a good thing; his imagination filled it in well enough anyway.

A group of three men standing by the edge of the road looked up as Jake approached. Of the three, two were wearing police uniforms; the other was wearing a dress shirt and tie, covered by a long overcoat. This man muttered something to the uniformed officers and they left to go do some other task. Then he approached Jake's car.

"Good evening, sir," Jake said, rolling down the window.

"This is the site of an ongoing investigation," said the man, ignoring Jake's greeting completely. His eyes narrowed as he looked at his watch and he added, "It's nearly midnight. What are you doing out so late?"

"I just got off work an hour ago. I thought I'd stop by my wife's grave on my way home."

"I'm sorry for your loss," the man in the overcoat muttered, averting his eyes and not sounding very sorry at all.

"Thank you," Jake said, just as stiffly.

"I'm afraid you'll have to turn around," he said, back to business once more. "Take the first left, then go left again on Main Street. You can get back on this road after you've passed the music shop two doors down."

He stalked away before Jake had a chance to say anything else.

CHAPTER 2

A few hours later Jake was at home, tired but unable to sleep. He couldn't help feeling a sort of morbid curiosity about what had happened at the crime scene he had passed. He paced around and around his small two-bedroom house, which was just one of many identical houses in this little suburban neighborhood.

He may not have been living in the lap of luxury, but neither was he living in total squalor. When all was said and done, it was a house of the perfect size and quality for a single man with a less-than-great education. College had only ever been a dream to begin with. But once he found out that his high school sweetheart, Margie, was pregnant with his child, college had been taken completely out of the question.

Instead of working two jobs to finance his education, Jake found himself working to support his new pregnant wife and himself. This had been the only place they could afford to rent that was in a relatively safe part of town. Not that it seemed that safe anymore. That murder—for Jake felt somehow sure that it had been a murder—had happened practically in his backyard. But the thought that was really tugging at him was wondering if he had known the victim. It wasn't that big of a town, so the possibility wasn't actually that far-fetched.

Perhaps he would stop by the flower store the next morning and ask Harry, the owner, if he knew what had happened. Maybe he had even heard or seen something. Jake's last thought before he fell asleep was, *The papers are going to have a field day with this one.* Things like this just didn't happen in small-town America.

* * *

As it turned out, Jake did not go see Harry the florist the next morning. Because he had slept so poorly, Jake didn't hear his alarm clock go off and woke up twenty minutes before his shift was supposed to start. There was no time for coffee, breakfast or even a shower. He just threw some clothes on, grabbed his keys and bolted out the door. And of course there was a thick layer of ice on his windshield. It took him several tries to start up the engine; even when it finally cranked over, the defroster took a long time to actually do its job.

"Can I just catch one break this morning?" Jake asked his empty car angrily. The engine shuddered in reply.

Apparently Jake would not be catching any breaks. Following his normal route to the power plant where he worked, Jake had to drive right past the crime scene where traffic was still being detoured. Then another section of the road was closed due to a burst water main, so he had to make another detour. With one thing and another, he ended up being nearly an hour late to work.

He had barely gotten to his workstation when Mike Levee, who worked next to him in the line, turned to him to offer more bad news.

"Boss said to send you up to his office as soon as you got here. You're probably gonna get it since you were late."

"You're one to talk," Jake snapped back, but without any real animosity. Mike was the closest friend he had in this town.

"Yeah, but I've been late so often it's pretty much expected by now," Mike replied. Jake almost laughed at how little concern he showed at this fact. "You on the other hand: you're always on time. It's a big deal when you're late. You'd better get going before you get in even more trouble."

"You're probably right," Jake said and headed upstairs to his boss's office. He knocked on the door and a voice told him to enter.

"You wanted to see me, sir?" Jake asked.

"Not me," answered Gary Plummer. "These two gentlemen." He indicated the two men occupying the chairs in front of his desk. As they rose and turned around to face the office door, Jake recognized one of them as the man he had spoken with at the crime scene the previous evening. If the man was also surprised to see Jake he was certainly better at hiding it.

"Hello, Mr. Henderson. I'm Detective Steve Braxton and this is my partner, Detective Mark Jordan." He indicated the tall, slim, dark-haired man standing next to him.

Jake shook hands with both of them and then asked, "What's this all about, detectives?"

"We'd like you to come downtown with us," Detective Jordan informed him. He offered no other explanation, which did nothing to relieve the knot that was currently growing in Jake's gut.

"All right," said Jake, hoping the tension in his stomach would not show on his face. "I'll just need to go and collect my things from my locker."

"We'll come with you," Detective Braxton said, donning his overcoat. "Thank you for all your help, Mr. Plummer."

As Jake led the two detectives downstairs to the break room, his mind was reeling. Given that he had seen Detective Braxton at the crime scene, it seemed logical that this had something to do with whatever had happened behind the flower shop last night. And their attitude—mainly the unwill-ingness to communicate any information—made him feel like a suspect.

Just play it cool, Jake, he thought. *You've done nothing wrong so you have absolutely nothing to hide.* So why were his fingers twitch-ing as he tried to get his locker open? They used to only shake like that when he was craving a hit of cocaine.

"Cold in here, isn't it?" Detective Braxton said, smiling in a rather unpleasant way.

Jake shrugged. "They have to keep the machines cool."

There was no further conversation as the detectives led Jake out of the building to their car. Sitting in the back seat behind the Plexiglass shield, Jake felt like he was under arrest. Finally, he found his voice.

"Have I done something wrong?" he asked.

"Guilty conscience, eh?" Braxton said from behind the wheel.

"Don't worry, Mr. Henderson, we're not accusing you of anything," Detective Jordan said, frowning at his partner. "We just want to talk to you privately and our station would be the best place to do that."

That still sounded like bad news to Jake, but he did feel a little bit better after Jordan's reassurance. Ten silent minutes later, they pulled into the parking lot behind the police station and got out of the car. Detectives Jordan and Braxton led the way up to the second floor of the building and into a small, rather cramped room lit by a bar of flickering fluorescent lights hanging from the ceiling. A bare wooden table took up most of the space; the only other pieces of furniture in the room were four metal chairs that surrounded the table, two on each side. And one of those chairs was already occupied.

CHAPTER 3

Jake froze when he saw who was sitting there. For the first time in nearly seven years, he looked into eyes that perfectly matched his own. The nose was Jake's as well, but the red-blond hair was Margie's.

"Hello, Griffin," Jake said after a moment.

"Hi Dad. Long time no see."

Griffin was tall and thin, as he had been growing up. But it was clear that he had taken up an interest in weight lifting since he had left home. His arms bulged beneath the sleeves of his T-shirt and Jake could see a tattoo of a snake on his left bicep. His hair was longer than Jake remembered it being and it looked like he used a fair amount of gel in it. Then there were the more subtle differences—like the fact that Griffin's face didn't look quite so worry-free anymore. There was fear and concern in equal measure behind his eyes. The fact was that, at twenty-eight, Griffin was no longer a child. He was a grown man; still young, still inexperienced, but with adult worries and cares riding on his shoulders.

A painful jolt went through Jake's heart as he realized that he had missed out on watching his son grow up. Even when Griffin had been living under Jake's roof, they had either ignored each other or argued almost every day since Margie died. He could see some of these same thoughts going through Griffin's mind as well. For almost a full minute they just looked at one another. Then, hesitantly, Jake held out his hand. Just as hesitantly, Griffin shook it. Jake would have liked to embrace him, but settled for clapping him on the shoulder with his free hand. It was an awkward gesture—and not well received to judge by the look on Griffin's face—but at least it was a step in the right direction.

Jake released his son's hand and then turned back to the two detectives, who had kept silent during this family reunion.

"I still don't understand why I'm here. Has Griffin done something wrong?"

"Nice how you just assume that, Dad," Griffin said, glaring at him and sounding very much like his old teenage self. "Besides, I'm an adult now. Even if I had done something wrong—which by the way I haven't—they would just throw me in jail and be done with it. They wouldn't call my father to come down to the police station and give me a lecture."

"If you're an adult, you could try acting like one," Jake replied. There was a frostiness to his voice that surprised even him. Was this any way to talk to someone he hadn't seen in years? Before Griffin could answer back, Detective Braxton closed the door loudly enough to effectively break up the argument.

"We're not here about Griffin," he said. "Now please, sit down."

Jake and Griffin sat down on one side of the table and the two detectives took the seats across from them.

"There's no easy way to say what I'm about to say," said Detective Braxton. He hesitated and then went on, "I'm sure you are both aware that somebody was killed last night, behind the flower shop on Main Street?"

Jake and Griffin both nodded.

"Well, we found a wallet and I.D. with the woman's body." Again, Braxton hesitated and then finally he just came out and said it. "The body was that of Anne Henderson."

Jake simply sat there looking at him. He didn't know what he had expected to hear, but it wasn't this. How could she be gone? There must be some kind of mistake. What would his sweet, innocent little girl be doing in a back parking lot alone at that time of night, anyway?

He couldn't speak; he couldn't even cry. He just felt numb, paralyzed. His hands twitched a little, but that was all the movement that he was capable of. He felt like a prisoner trapped inside his own body with all the emotions running through him. Dimly, he heard someone sobbing.

For a moment, Jake thought his internal grief had broken loose. But it was Griffin. It suddenly occurred to Jake that he had never really seen his son break down like this. If he had done it after his mother died then it must have been when Jake was too drunk or high to take any notice. Jake reached over and rubbed his son's back; it was the only way he could think of to comfort him. When Griffin became aware of this, which took quite a bit of time, he immediately shook Jake's hand off, and refused to take the handkerchief he was offering. In fact, he didn't even look at his father. Instead, he looked at the two men sitting across the table.

"How can she be dead?" he asked hoarsely, wiping his eyes with his sleeve. "There must be some kind of mistake."

"There was no mistake. We're positive that it's her," Detective Jordan said in a soft voice. "Both of you have my sincerest condolences."

"Can I see her?" Jake asked, looking up at the two detectives and hating the way his voice shook even though he knew he had every reason in the world to be upset.

"Why? Feeling guilty that you haven't spoken to her in the last eight years?" Griffin said in a hard voice.

"I'll see if the medical examiner will allow it," Detective Jordan offered and left the room. There was a very loaded silence while he was gone.

"She's expecting us," he said when he returned a few minutes later. "The morgue is just down the road a ways. I'll take you there when you're ready."

Without looking at his son, Jake rose and followed Jordan from the room.

CHAPTER 4

The morgue turned out to be in the basement of a plain brick building three doors down from the police station. When Jordan and Jake got to the bottom of the stairs they turned left down a long white hallway toward a pair of wooden doors at the end. Although there was nothing in that hallway to inspire fear, it was a terrifying walk for Jake. As he approached the doors, he became aware that his heart was beating faster and harder than he could ever remember it beating before.

Detective Jordan pushed open the doors and Jake saw that there was another door a few yards away with a large pane of viewing glass in it. Through that window, Jake could see a woman in scrubs standing next to a waist-high metal table. On the table was a body covered with a sheet. Jake stopped abruptly and Jordan looked back at him with empathy and compassion in his eyes. He moved slightly so that his head blocked the glass at the top of the door.

"Are you sure you want to do this, Mr. Henderson?"

Jake almost called the whole thing off right then and there. But a moment later he felt sickened with himself. What kind of selfish cowardice was that? He couldn't imagine what Anne must have gone through, the pain she had suffered. And he couldn't bear to put himself through just a little?

"No," Jake said slowly. "I don't want to do this. But I need to. I owe her that much."

Jordan looked back at him and nodded, unsmiling. Then he said, "When I give the word to the medical examiner she'll pull the sheet back so you can see the head. You can look for as long or as short a time as you want. Just…tell me when you're ready."

Jake didn't think he would ever be truly ready but he took a deep breath to cleanse his mind and steel his nerves. Then he nodded.

The two men walked slowly forward until they came to the door with the window and Jake closed his eyes as Detective Jordan gave the signal to the woman in scrubs.

When Jake opened his eyes and raised his head, the world around him seemed to just melt away. All he could see was his daughter's face. It was much easier to look at her than he had expected. When Margie died it had been worse; Jake had barely even recognized her. That was not the case with Anne. How many times had he looked in on her after she had fallen asleep as a child? She almost looked that way now, so peaceful, with her long blonde hair spilling out around her. The only thing that ruined it was the fact that her hair seemed strangely matted in the back. Jake thought he knew why and felt his stomach clench.

But he only turned away when he felt a sharp prick behind his eyes.

"I've seen enough," he said, and was relieved to find that his voice was actually fairly steady. "Thank you."

Glancing up, Jake saw Detective Jordan nod to the medical examiner once more. Then the two of them started back down the hallway toward the stairs. There was silence between them until Jake glimpsed a restroom they were passing.

"Do you mind if I take a few minutes in here?" he asked. "I just want to splash my face with some cold water."

"Take all the time you need," said the young detective in that reassuring way he had. "I'll be right outside."

Jake thanked him and then entered the mercifully empty restroom. Locking himself into the handicapped stall, he slid down the wall until he was sitting on the cold tile. He forced himself to keep sitting there and taking deep breaths until he had calmed down considerably; still, it took a concentrated effort to stop his tears completely. When he had finished crying he used the bathroom and washed his hands in the sink.

Finally, he splashed himself in the face with cold water. It was incredibly refreshing. As he was drying off with a paper towel, he stared at his eyes in the mirror. Those couldn't possibly be his eyes, could they? Not those dead-looking, haunted things? Jake forced himself to look away before the tears could threaten to start again.

16

Taking one more calming breath, Jake tossed his used paper towels in the trash can and walked back out into the hallway. Detective Jordan was leaning against the wall in the exact same position Jake had left him in. Jake wondered vaguely and without much interest whether he had even moved. Without speaking, Jake turned to continue back down the hallway toward the stairs; Detective Jordan fell easily into step beside him.

As they were walking, Jake asked, "What happened to her exactly? And who would want to do this to my little girl?"

"I think that's something we should all discuss once we get back to the station," the detective replied. "I'm sure your son has the same questions."

Jake felt a sharp twinge of regret that Jordan had thought of that and not him. How could he have forgotten his son so easily? There was no further conversation as they made their way back down the street and up to the room on the second floor of the police station where Griffin was waiting with Detective Braxton. Griffin glanced at his father and then looked away just as quickly. But in that brief moment, Jake saw that the same haunted look in his eyes was also in the eyes of his son.

Jake sat down in the chair beside Griffin and said, "Please, tell us what happened to her." His voice was hoarse but otherwise sounded very calm.

Detective Braxton extracted a notebook from the inside of his suit jacket and flipped through it before speaking. "At approximately 9:45 yesterday evening, emergency dispatch received an anonymous tip that a crime had been committed behind the flower shop where Anne was found. Responding officers immediately contacted paramedics, but all efforts to resuscitate the victim were unsuccessful. The exact cause of death is still being determined, but we will keep you informed of any developments."

"Did she suffer?" Griffin asked. His voice sounded detached, almost uncaring. But his eyes revealed the truth: the tough exterior was nothing more than a wall put up to hide his emotions.

"Nobody can answer that for sure except her attacker," Detective Jordan said. "But I'm afraid that yes, she probably did suffer."

"Do you have any suspects?" Griffin asked. His tone was accusatory, as though he thought the detectives weren't doing their jobs properly.

"We were hoping the two of you might be able to help us with that," Detective Braxton said, reaching back inside his jacket and this time producing a pencil. "Did Anne have any enemies? Anyone at all who might have wanted her dead?"

"No," Jake said immediately. "She was always so kind to everybody."

"You haven't seen her in a long time, Dad," Griffin reminded him. He didn't even raise his head to look his father in the eyes; he addressed the corner of the table instead. "You have no idea what she was like."

Jake opened his mouth to argue but found there was nothing he could say.

"You're right," he said. Griffin was so surprised he actually looked up. "Weren't expecting that, were you? But you are right. And believe me, if I could go back and change that then I would. I would spend more time with you and her both. But as it stands, I guess I just have a hard time believing that she could change so completely from when she was younger."

"Are you suggesting your father's impression of his daughter is wrong, Griffin?" Detective Jordan asked. "Did Anne have any bad habits that we should know about?

"You mean anything that would have caused her to be lurking alone behind a closed store in an empty parking lot at night?" Griffin sighed and then said, "No. My dad's right. She was a good person."

"So you can't think of anyone?" Detective Braxton sounded disappointed.

"Well, there was her boyfriend. Some guy named Karl," Griffin said. "Ex-boyfriend I guess; they broke up a little over a week ago."

"Do you know the last name?" Detective Braxton asked, his pencil zipping across the page in front of him.

"She didn't mention one, but he spelled his name with a K, not with a C."

"How do you know?"

"I met Anne for lunch last week and a text message popped up from him on her phone."

"Last week…that would be about the time they broke up?" Detective Jordan guessed, raising an eyebrow.

"Yes. She admitted that things hadn't been going so well between them and they had just broken up the night before."

"Do you know what caused the break-up? I mean, could it possibly have been an abusive relationship?" Braxton asked, flipping to a clean page and twirling his pencil around in his fingers.

"I never met the guy, so I can't really say," said Griffin.

"No," Jake said at the same time. In response to Detective Jordan's questioning look, Jake explained, "When she was sixteen, she helped a friend of hers get out of an abusive relationship. After seeing what it does to somebody, I highly doubt she would get herself into that kind of situation."

"Helping a friend isn't the same as helping yourself," said Griffin. He acted like he was speaking to nobody in particular but Jake knew that comment was really directed at him. Nevertheless, he refrained from arguing back. There were more important things to worry about at the moment.

After a few seconds of awkward silence, the two detectives exchanged a look. It was only a quick look, but it was enough.

"Thank you for all your help," said Detective Braxton, getting to his feet. The other three men followed suit. Braxton reached into another pocket and fished out two business cards. He handed one each to Jake and Griffin, saying, "If you think of anything else that could help us, please get in touch."

"Of course," said Jake. He tucked the card into his pocket and shook hands with both detectives.

"If you'll follow me," said Detective Jordan, "I can give you both a ride back to where your vehicles are."

"Thank you," said Jake, as they all made their way out of the interview room and started downstairs.

"If it's all the same to you, I'd prefer to take the bus," Griffin said. "I just need some time to myself and walking to the bus stop sounds like the perfect way to clear my head."

"Are you sure? I have plenty of room to take both of you."

"I'm sure," said Griffin. By this point they had reached the front door of the building. "Thank you, detectives. See you around I guess, Dad," he added after a pause.

"Yeah," said Jake; he felt very drained all of a sudden. "Be safe, okay?"

"Course I will."

He walked away without saying anything else. As Jake and Detective Jordan got in the car and pulled out of the parking lot, Jake watched as his son vanished in the rearview mirror.

CHAPTER 5

Ten minutes later, Detective Jordan dropped Jake off at the power plant. He reminded him once again to call if he thought of anything that might help the investigation and then left him standing in the snow beside his car.

Jake got in his car and started it up. It took a few seconds but the engine finally caught. Jake shifted into reverse and then stopped. He turned off the engine and walked inside the building.

"Hey Jake!" Mike Levee called to him from across the room. "What happened, man?"

Jake didn't reply; he barely even heard him. He walked upstairs to his boss's office and knocked on the door in a daze.

"Come in," a bored voice called from within.

Jake did as the voice asked him to. When Gary Plummer looked up and saw who it was, his face immediately registered sympathy.

"You don't need to say anything, Jake," he said, putting his hand up as Jake opened his mouth. "The police told me what happened when they came earlier. I don't know what to say, other than I'm sorry."

"Thank you," Jake said. His voice was mechanical, barely recognizable as his own.

"Why don't you have a seat?"

Jake sank down into one of the chairs in front of the desk.

"What did they talk to you about?"

"Just establishing your character. Were you a good worker, what your attendance was like, that sort of thing."

But Jake thought there was something his boss was leaving out.

"I suppose they were particularly interested in my attendance last night?"

"Yes, they were," Mr. Plummer admitted with a sigh. "But you can't think they actually consider you a suspect, Jake. You know how it is with these things; they always investigate the family members first."

"To be honest, I don't really know what to think right now," said Jake. "I just want to get home and get some rest. After that I might be able to think more clearly."

Jake got up and was halfway to the door before he remembered why he had come up here in the first place.

"Would it be alright if I took a few days off?" he asked.

"You take as much time as you need. We'll all be thinking about you in the meantime."

"Thanks," said Jake. It was all he could manage. Then he turned and hurried back downstairs and out to his car. He noted that the wind seemed to be particularly cold on his cheeks. Raising a hand to his face he was unsurprised to find fresh tear tracks there.

He leaned forward and rested his forehead on the steering wheel; he allowed himself exactly ten seconds to give in to everything he was feeling. When that time had expired he straightened up, ran the sleeve of his coat across his face and drove home, taking a route that completely avoided the flower shop. He called it the flower shop because he couldn't bear to call it what it really was: the crime scene. The last thing his daughter's eyes had seen before she died.

When Jake pulled into his driveway it took him a few seconds to realize that there was a man pacing on his front porch. The man turned his head when he heard the car and as Jake realized who it was, he felt pure anger rise up inside him, burning away the pain and grief. He welcomed the numbness it brought.

Jake switched off the ignition, got out of the car and slammed the door with as much force as he could.

"Get out of here, Tony," he said without preamble, crossing the snowy yard and getting right in the man's face.

"Look, I wouldn't be here if I didn't have a good reason," said Tony, running a sweaty, shaky hand through his greasy hair.

"No reason you could come up with could possibly be good," Jake said with a snort of humorless laughter. "In case you've forgotten, I'm through with all the so-called services you offer."

"It's not about that, man, I swear," Tony said, putting up his hands in a gesture of surrender; Jake still had not backed away from him.

"I'm warning you, Tony," said Jake, with no idea of how he was going to follow up the vague threat.

"I saw someone last night. Someone you might be interested in. Please, man, just listen to me."

"Shut up," said Jake, shoving Tony backward. It wasn't a particularly hard push but it was still enough to make Tony fall off the porch and land sprawling on the front lawn. Jake took advantage of the situation and unlocked his front door.

He looked back over his shoulder as he stepped inside and said, "If I see you anywhere near here again, I won't hesitate to call the police. Now leave."

With that, he slammed the door behind him and locked it. His hand still resting on the knob, he looked through the peephole and watched until Tony had struggled to his feet and skulked off. When he was gone, Jake wandered to the small kitchen table and sat down, staring into space and thinking.

He spared a little bit of curiosity about why his old dealer would suddenly decide to stop by to pay him a visit. But mostly he thought about all the times he had shared with Anne, all the times that they could have shared but didn't. After a little while he got up and walked into his bedroom where he lay down without bothering to undress. Before he knew it, he had drifted off to sleep.

CHAPTER 6

Detective Jordan had barely reached his desk back at the police precinct when Detective Braxton came over.

"Captain wants an update," he said.

"We just started," Jordan replied, tossing his coat over the back of his chair. "What the hell kind of progress does he expect us to have made?"

Braxton just shrugged; it was his way of showing sympathy but he couldn't say anything because they were walking into Captain Huntington's office. The captain looked up as he heard them come in. He motioned for them to close the door and be quiet; then he finished his phone call and hung up.

"So," he said, leaning back in his chair and interlocking his fingers behind his head. "What do you gentlemen have so far?"

"According to the victim's brother she broke up with her boyfriend about a week ago," Detective Jordan began.

"We're working on tracking him down but all we have is a first name, so it's proving to be difficult," Braxton added.

"That's it?" asked the captain. The tone in his voice made it clear that he had expected more. "What about the family?"

"Mother died ten years ago; sounds like things were pretty strained in the house after that. The father really wasn't much help at all."

"Well he wouldn't be if he's the one that killed her," said Braxton.

Jordan glared at him. There was no denying that his partner was a good cop, but he had a flair for the dramatic which was particularly annoying because it always seemed to paint Detective Jordan in the worst light. *Always trying to show me up just because he has a little bit more experience than I do. Sometimes I think he forgets we both hold the same title.*

"I'm assuming you have some evidence to back up that claim, Detective?" asked Captain Huntington. He was well aware of Braxton's tendencies toward dramatics.

"We ran his name through the system. Turns out he has a little problem with cocaine. He was arrested six years ago and sentenced to a mandatory drug rehab program."

"And did he complete the program?" the captain probed.

"Well yes," Braxton replied, dismissing this fact with a wave of his hand. "But that's not exactly a guarantee for staying clean, now is it?"

"I've spent more time with him than you have," Detective Jordan chimed in. "He didn't act like he was looking for a fix."

"Maybe he's gotten one recently."

"Did he look like he was high to you?"

"He did seem pretty out of it, now that you mention it." Braxton's tone made it clear that he had been hoping Detective Jordan would bring up this very point.

"Cocaine wouldn't make you act that way. Although maybe the fact that he just lost his daughter had something to do with it," said Jordan with the air of somebody making a great discovery.

"He certainly didn't seem very upset. His son on the other hand—"

"His son seemed too upset," said Jordan. "Did you notice how he kept his face hidden the entire time he was 'crying'? Maybe he was trying to hide the fact that he wasn't actually crying. Maybe he was just proud of the good work he had done."

"Or maybe the fact that he just lost his older sister had something to do with it."

"All right, that's enough," said the captain, when he had ascertained that the argument between partners was not going to lead anywhere productive. "Both of you work on tracking down the boyfriend. If he checks out, then you can chase your own leads. Get to work and keep me posted."

Jordan waited until they had gotten back to the main squad room before rounding on his partner. "Nice of you to share that bit of information with me about the father."

"Look, you have to admit it's suspicious," Braxton said.

"He seemed like he knew nothing about his daughter though," Jordan said, frowning. "His son certainly kept throwing that fact in his face. You really think it makes sense that he would track her down after all these years and kill her?"

"Does a motive for murder ever make sense?"

Detective Jordan could think of no response to that so he turned to his computer and pulled up the search results for the first name Karl. Even with the unusual spelling, the list was several pages long. He let out a long sigh of frustration.

"Looks like it's going to be a long night."

"We need something to narrow it down," said Braxton, who was looking over his partner's shoulder at the computer screen.

"Griffin said Anne got a text from him last week. That would give us his number. We could just give him a call and have him come to us."

Braxton looked rather unhappy that Jordan had come up with that idea before him. There was a slight hitch, however; a visit to the evidence locker turned up no cell phone.

"Why would the killer take her phone but not her wallet?" Jordan asked. "I mean, let's say I was a cold-blooded murderer. If I was going to steal something from somebody I had just killed then I would want to make it harder for the police to identify the body."

"He probably knew the phone would point the finger at him. Or maybe she just wasn't carrying her phone with her."

"Come on," Jordan half-laughed, giving his partner a look. "Every twenty-something year old has their phone attached to their ear."

"I think it's time we checked out Anne's apartment. Maybe we'll find her cell phone there."

The two headed back to the squad room to pick up their coats and then drove to the address listed on Anne's driver's license.

CHAPTER 7

It was an apartment building on Caster Street, one of three on the block.

"Let's go see if the landlord can help us out with getting a key," Braxton said as they got out of the car. They walked inside the building and showed their badges to the man sitting behind the desk.

"We need to speak to the superintendent, please," Jordan said.

"That's me. Bill Horowitz. What can I help you guys with?"

"We need a key to Anne Henderson's apartment."

Mr. Horowitz tapped a few keys on his computer. After a minute he said triumphantly, "Unit 307. I'll walk you up there."

Unit 307 contained a tiny kitchen, a bedroom, and a living room that was only large enough to hold a loveseat and an entertainment center with a small TV on it.

"We can take it from here, Mr. Horowitz," Braxton said. It was just shy of being a direct dismissal.

32

"Actually, before you go," Jordan said, pulling out a note-book. Braxton scowled at the contradiction but let it pass and continued into the bedroom. "Can you tell me whether Anne had anyone over to visit in the past couple of days?"

"No, she didn't. She was one of our quietest tenants, never gave any trouble. Kept herself to herself except for that boy that came over sometimes. Haven't seen him in a while, though."

"What boy?" Jordan asked.

"Tall, thin, blonde hair. Tattoo of a snake on his arm. I assumed it was her boyfriend."

"Thanks. Oh, and if he comes asking for her, please let us know right away." He handed over his business card and went to join his partner in Anne's bedroom. It was very neat; the books on the shelf were all in alphabetical order, and the hangers in the closet all faced the same direction. Braxton was looking at a picture on the nightstand of a very pretty woman with long red-blonde hair.

"I imagine that would be the mother?" Jordan asked.

"I'd imagine so. Did you get anything useful from our friend the superintendent?"

"Griffin was a frequent visitor. Not recently though."

"Interesting. You know another thing that's interesting? No phone. There's the charger there, see. But no phone."

"That certainly makes it seem like she had it with her when she was killed," Jordan said slowly.

"So where is it now?"

Before they had time to discuss it any further, Braxton's cell phone rang. He answered it, and his face fell as he listened to whoever was on the other end of the line.

"Got it. We'll be right there," he said and hung up. "That was the captain. We've got another crime scene to go to."

"I thought he wanted us to give our full attention to this case."

"That's why he sent other officers to go check it out at first. They canvassed the neighborhood and one lady saw the murder victim arguing with her neighbor—one Jacob Henderson."

Without another word, Braxton led the way downstairs and out of the building.

* * *

The second murder victim was slumped against a brick wall, his eyes still half-open and an expression of surprise on his face.

"Do we know who this guy is?" Jordan asked a passing officer.

"There was no I.D. But we're checking his fingerprints right now to see if he's in the system. And we found a cell phone in his hand but it probably wasn't his."

"What makes you say that?" Braxton inquired.

"Somehow he doesn't strike me as the type of guy who would use a bright pink case with flowers on it."

34

She handed them the evidence bag that contained the phone and strode off to continue processing the crime scene.

Jordan pulled out the phone with a gloved hand and started scrolling through it.

"What are you looking for?"

"Some kind of evidence that would help us determine who this phone really belongs to. But there's nothing. All the data's been wiped off of it."

"But I think we both know whose phone it is anyway," Braxton said.

"You're thinking it's Anne's," Jordan replied.

"This murder has to be connected to the one from last night. Why else would Jake be arguing the him?"

"Let's find out who this guy is first before we jump to any conclusions."

"Tony Mazarria," said the officer they'd spoken to earlier, coming over to them. "He's got a rap sheet a mile long, all drug-related charges."

"I suppose that explains the argument with our friend Mr. Henderson," Braxton said; he couldn't quite keep the satisfaction out of his voice. "I think we should just arrest him right now."

"Based on what, the fact that they had a disagreement? I can think of a lot of people who have a reason to argue with a drug dealer."

"You can't say it isn't suspicious."

"I think it's a little too neat," Jordan said thoughtfully. "The location, the showy way the cell phone was placed…to me that looks like somebody's trying to frame Jake for murder."

Something in his partner's tone made Braxton look over at him.

"You think you know who that someone might be?"

"I don't feel comfortable saying just yet," Jordan answered.

"So I'll say it for you. You think it's Griffin."

"I think you suspect him, too."

"And what makes you think that?" But Braxton didn't deny it.

"I saw how closely you were watching him while he was walking toward the bus stop."

"I just think it's a cold day to go for a walk and clear your head."

"You said you ran Jake's name through the system; did you run Griffin's as well?"

"Yes. And he was clean as a whistle," Braxton said. "Which makes Jake Henderson a better fit."

Jordan didn't want to admit it but Braxton did have a point. "Let's at least go have a word with the captain before we decide what to do next."

So they got in their car and drove back to the station, each forming their arguments for the person they thought was guilty. When they arrived they went straight up to their captain's office.

"So tell me your thoughts about the death of Mr. Mazarria," Huntington said when they had both sat down.

"We are in agreement that the same person committed both crimes," Braxton told their captain before Jordan had a chance to speak. "But we disagree about who that person is. I suspect Jake Henderson, for reasons I feel are obvious."

"And I think Griffin Henderson did it," Jordan put in.

Captain Huntington thought for a minute before saying, "Do we even know that this cell phone belonged to Anne?"

"No," said Jordan. "It's been sent to forensics but it's going to take at least a day before they can identify the prints that were on it.

"Here's what I want you to do, since you can't seem to agree on who to pursue. Call father and son both in here, but separately. Push them both hard and see how they react; that should give us some insight about who might be guilty. But there's another suspect you're both forgetting."

"Karl. Right," Braxton said. He really had forgotten about him.

"Yes. While you two have been out at the crime scenes, I've had other detectives looking into this man with no last name. We're making some progress, but I still have about ten people that need to be interviewed. I'll expect your help after you're done with the family."

"Of course," both detectives said.

"Good. Now get back to work. Use your best judgment about whether to question Jake or Griffin first."

CHAPTER 8

Griffin stared at the number on his cell phone. *What do the cops want now?* He debated just letting it go to voicemail and then deciding whether or not to return the call. Then again, they might take that the wrong way. On the last ring, he picked it up.

"Hello?"

"Hello, Griffin. This is Detective Braxton, we met this morning?"

"Yeah, I remember you. You're not someone I'm likely to forget anytime soon."

"An unfortunate fact of the job. Can you come back in to the station? We have a few more questions for you."

"You can't just ask them over the phone?" Griffin asked, looking at his watch. It had been a long day, and all he wanted to do was sleep.

"No, I think it's best we ask them in person."

Again Griffin hesitated before replying. "All right. I'll drive over there now."

"We look forward to it. Just ask for me or my partner when you get here."

Griffin hung up without bothering to say goodbye. Trying to ignore the itching anxiety he was feeling, he grabbed his coat and headed out the door.

Braxton met him in the lobby of the station and brought him upstairs straight away, but to a different room this time.

"Someone watching from behind that glass?" Griffin asked, looking at the mirror on the wall.

"Not at the moment," Braxton answered. But this was a lie. Detective Jordan was outside listening to every word.

"What questions do you have, Detective?"

"We wanted to know some more about this man Karl that you mentioned earlier. Did your sister ever mention what he did, where he lived, anything like that?"

"No," Griffin said and then changed his tune. "Wait, yes. She said he was a cameraman on some film project that she was going to be working on, said he helped her get the job. That's what Anne did; she was an actress. I took some classes myself but she was always the star of the show."

"Do you know the title of this film? Or the location where it was being shot?"

"I can't remember the title, but I know it was being filmed in New York."

"Thank you," Braxton said, writing down the information. "That's going to help us out a lot."

"I'm just sorry I didn't think of it earlier; it would have saved me another trip down here." Griffin did a fairly decent job of hiding the annoyance in his voice but Braxton still picked up on it. "Anything else I can help you with?"

"Yes, as a matter of fact. Do you recognize this?"

He held up a picture of the pink cell phone that they had found with the drug dealer's body. Griffin's face fell as he looked at it.

"That's my sister's phone."

"Are you sure?"

"Positive. But if you found her phone then why don't you just look up Karl's number, give him a call and have him come to you?"

"Because we can't get the information we need from Anne's phone; it's gone."

"Gone?" Griffin repeated.

"Yes. The killer must have wiped it clean of all information before he dumped it. Still, it's really a stroke of luck that we found it. Our forensics team will be able to determine who did the wiping and that will tell us who killed her."

"That's good news," Griffin said, not quite making eye contact. "But it still doesn't explain why you hauled me in here to ask me questions about her ex-boyfriend. If you're so confident in your forensics techs, surely you believe they can recover some of the lost data?"

"We didn't 'haul you in here' as you phrased it. I thought I was actually being quite polite when I asked you to come down here to talk."

"Like I had any real choice in the matter," Griffin snapped.

"Well, you're not under arrest so you're free to leave at any time," Braxton told him.

"Good," Griffin replied, rising from his chair.

"Just one more question before you go: do you know someone named Tony Mazarria?"

"Who's that?" Griffin asked, his hand on the doorknob. But Braxton thought he said it just a little too quickly, and his eyes flicked down and to the left. Still, he pretended to notice nothing.

"Just another name that came up. That's all right, though."

"Sorry I couldn't be of any more help," Griffin said sarcastically. "Looks like you'll have to do your job all by yourself."

And he left, slamming the door behind him.

Once Griffin was gone, Braxton entered the observation room next door where Detective Jordan was standing.

"He's lying," Jordan said without hesitation.

"About the drug dealer, yes. But is he lying about Karl, too? Because if he is, then we might be chasing a ghost."

"I guess for now we'll just have to assume that he's real," Jordan said. "Go tell the others the updated info about Karl."

"Why me?" Braxton asked; he disliked being ordered about by his younger partner.

"Because I have another interview to schedule."

41

EMILY DAVIDSON

* * *

Jake wasn't sure how long he had been asleep when he was awakened by a ringing in his ears. It took his sleep-fogged mind a few seconds to realize that the ringing was coming from the phone in his kitchen. He got to his feet and stumbled to the bedroom door. Clearly he had been asleep at least long enough for his muscles to stiffen up.

By the time he made it to the phone, he had missed the call. But now that he was in the kitchen he realized he was starving. He glanced at his watch and saw that it was half past six in the evening. *Why have I been sleeping in the middle of the day? Why didn't I go to work?* Then everything came rushing back to him and he no longer felt remotely tired; instead he was wide awake and filled with fear and pain. Jake stood there rocking back and forth in the middle of his kitchen, his eyes shut tight. He counted to ten very slowly, then opened his eyes and started gathering the necessary ingredients for a sandwich.

Only when he had eaten half of it did he turn his attention to the phone. As he had expected, the light on the receiver was blinking red, telling him that he had a message. Jake took the phone out of its cradle and dialed his voice mailbox.

"Please enter your password," the machine informed him. Jake did as the voice requested.

"You have one new message. To play your messages, press one." Jake pressed one before the machine had time to go through the rest of its automated spiel. The machine gave him the date, time and callback number and then the message began to roll.

"Mr. Henderson, this is Detective Mark Jordan. We need you to come back into the station as soon as possible. Please call me back as soon as you get this message. Thank you." He rattled off his phone number and then the machine's automated voice kicked in once more.

"To repeat this message, press one. To change your greeting, press three. To delete this message and go to the next, press seven. To save, press nine."

Jake punched the number seven and then hung up the phone. He put off calling the police as long as possible; he hadn't liked the tone of Detective Jordan's voice. But when he had finished his meal and taken care of the dishes—a task he dragged out for as long as he could—he knew he could not procrastinate any longer. He dug Jordan's business card out of his pocket and dialed the number. It was picked up on the first ring.

"Detective Jordan."

"Hello, Detective. This is Jake Henderson, I was just returning your call."

"Oh, thank you for getting back to me so quickly. Did you listen to the message I left?"

"Yes. I guess there's no way this can wait until the morning?"

"It would be best to talk as soon as possible," Jordan answered and all the warmth seeped out of his voice. "Time is of the essence in these kinds of situations, you know?"

Jake didn't know, especially since he wasn't sure exactly what kind of situation the detective was talking about. But he did know that arguing would be a complete waste of time.

"All right. I'll head over there as soon as I get off the phone."

"Wonderful. Just ask for myself or Detective Braxton when you get here." He hung up before Jake had a chance to say goodbye.

Jake used the drive over to the police station to compose his emotions and get himself under control. Just as he had that morning—had it really only been that morning? It seemed like so long ago—Jake felt a guilty, squirming knot in the pit of his stomach. But why should he? He had done absolutely nothing wrong. He'd been asleep the entire afternoon.

Why am I being treated like a criminal when I'm the victim? he wondered. But then he reminded himself, *No. Anne was the victim, not me. And I'm going to do whatever it takes to help the police catch her killer.*

With this attitude in mind, Jake pulled into the police station parking lot and went inside. He gave his name and both detectives' names to the woman sitting behind the reception desk. She made a phone call, her eyes on her watch and her nails drumming out a rhythm on the desktop.

"One of them will be out here in a minute, hon," she told him as she hung up the phone. "Just take a seat."

"Oh, thank you," said Jake. He sat down in a chair near the door and the receptionist proceeded to ignore him completely. Her drumming fingers and the irritated little sighs she made as she watched the clock were the only sounds in the room. Jake leaned his head back against the glass behind him and fell to wondering once again why he had been called here. He didn't have long to wait before Detective Jordan came out and led him back to the main squad room. Jordan shuffled through some papers on his desk until he found a thin manila folder. There was a name printed on it but Jordan covered it up with his finger so that Jake couldn't see what it said.

"With me, please."

Jake merely nodded and followed along in the young detective's wake until they reached an interview room. It was almost identical to the one Jake had been in earlier that day, but there were two additions that set it apart: a camera in the corner, near the ceiling, and a tape recorder in the middle of the table. It was strange how much the atmosphere in the room changed just because of those two things—more interrogation than interview. Detective Braxton was already waiting for them, slumped back in his seat. He straightened up as they entered and motioned for Jake to sit across from him. Jake did so, noting that the camera was focused on him. Detective Jordan had only just closed the door when Detective Braxton leaned forward over the table and began speaking.

"Let's just cut to the chase, Mr. Henderson. Why did you do it?"

"What exactly am I supposed to have done, Detective?"

"Oh nothing. Just killed somebody."

Jake almost laughed; anyone who knew him could testify that he was reluctant to kill so much as a spider. He could never take the life of another human being. But something told him that laughing might be the wrong reaction, so he sat back and said, "I don't understand, sir."

"Mr. Henderson," Detective Jordan asked, taking over from his partner, "where were you this afternoon? Say, about an hour after I dropped you off."

"I talked to my boss to explain what had happened and ask for some time off. Then I drove home and went to bed. It was your phone call that woke me up."

"Can anyone vouch for your whereabouts?" Braxton asked.

"Mike Levee can," Jake said after a moment's thought. "He spoke to me in passing as I walked inside the factory. And my boss Gary Plummer could tell you that I spoke with him."

"What about after you left the factory?" Braxton demanded, smacking the eraser end of his pencil against the table.

Jake hesitated for a fraction of a second before he remembered the vow he'd made with himself to be completely honest. Despite being so brief, the pause was enough to make Braxton's eyes narrow. Jake looked straight into those narrowed eyes as he spoke.

"When I first got home, there was someone waiting for me on the porch. His name's Tony Mazarria." Jake thought he saw a flash of triumph in Braxton's eyes but it was quickly disguised. "We talked for a minute, then I told him to leave and went inside. I'm afraid that only my bed can vouch for my whereabouts after that."

"So how do you know this guy Tony?" Jordan asked. But his tone suggested that he already knew the answer to that question.

Jake shifted his eyes over to Jordan and said, "Shortly after my wife died, I started using drugs." At this point his shame made him drop his eyes to his hands, which were clasped in front of him on the table. Then he looked up again and continued, "Tony was my primary supplier."

"You said the two of you talked for a minute. What did you talk about?" Detective Jordan asked him. He registered no surprise at hearing that Jake had been involved with drugs.

Jake thought for a minute, replaying the conversation in his head. He wanted to make sure he represented things as accurately as possible.

"When I saw who it was, I immediately asked him to leave," he began. "He said he had a good reason for coming there; I disagreed with him and told him I no longer needed his services. I haven't needed them since I went to rehab." If the two detectives already knew he'd been into drugs then they probably knew about the rehab as well, but Jake thought it would be best for him to emphasize this fact.

"Did he explain what his reason was for coming there?" Detective Jordan prompted him.

"He said he wanted to tell me about someone he saw last night. Said I might find it interesting. I told him that if I saw him at my house again, I wouldn't hesitate to call the police. Then I went inside."

"I think you're leaving something out, Mr. Henderson," said Braxton, with a grim smile on his face. "You see, we talked to your neighbor across the street and she said things got a little bit heated between you two."

Jake sighed and then said, "At one point—it was after he said he saw someone I might be interested in—I told him to shut up and I pushed him. I just wanted him to get out of my face so I could get inside and grab some sleep. It wasn't a hard push, but he lost his balance and fell backwards off the porch. But he was fine. He didn't even hit his head or anything."

"Oh we know. Your neighbor saw him walk off after you went inside."

"So, what's the problem?" asked Jake, but he had a bad feeling about where this was going. He didn't like the look on Braxton's face or the way it made his heart beat just a little bit faster.

"Tony's dead," Detective Jordan said abruptly, opening the envelope he had taken from his desk. He took out a picture and placed it on the table. The picture showed Tony Mazarria slumped against a brick wall, his eyes half open. Jake grimaced and looked away from it.

"I still don't understand what this has to do with me."

"Come on, Jake, you're a smart guy," Jordan said, although his tone was certainly not complimentary. "Put two and two together. You were the last person to see him alive. He was found in the shopping center two blocks from your house."

"And there's also that fact that your daughter's cell phone was found in his coat pocket," Braxton said, taking over for his partner.

The mention of Anne's cell phone hit Jake like a physical blow. "Why would he have her phone?"

"Well you're the one who put it there. Why don't you tell us?" Jordan suggested.

"What?" Jake said, looking up in total disbelief. "Why would I have her phone? I haven't seen her in over eight years."

"Why don't you sit tight and think about things for a while, Jake?" Braxton said, getting up and gesturing for his partner to do the same. "We'll be back in a few."

They left Jake to bury his head in his hands and try to fit all the pieces together. Why would a drug dealer have his daughter's phone? He had a hard time believing that Anne had been involved with anyone of that sort but a drug deal gone wrong would explain her death. And as Griffin had been quick to point out, Jake didn't know who his daughter had grown up to be. Now, thanks to whoever had killed her, he would never get the chance to reconnect.

And suddenly all the pieces slammed into place inside his head. The tone in Detective Jordan's voice over the phone, Braxton's little insinuation at the beginning of the interview, and his last statement: *you're the one who put it there.*

They thought he was the murderer. Not just the man who had killed Tony, but the man who had killed his own daughter.

"I didn't kill her," he whispered. And he shut his eyes and kept repeating this phrase to himself as he sat back and waited for the detectives to return.

CHAPTER 9

Outside, an argument was quickly becoming heated between Mark Jordan and Steve Braxton.

"What are your thoughts, Mark?"

"I don't think he did it. And don't bother telling me you do, you've made that more than clear already."

"He has a criminal record," Braxton said, spreading his hands in disbelief that Jordan wasn't grasping the obvious. "You honestly think his word is reliable? Because right now his word is all we've got."

"Exactly," Jordan said, taking a step closer to his partner. Braxton did not back down. "At this point, everything is hearsay. We have no concrete evidence one way or the other. Besides, I think—ah, never mind. It's not like you'll listen to me anyway." Jordan turned away from his partner and walked over to the window. He watch the cars go by on the street below with his hands cupped around his elbows.

Braxton heaved an impressive sigh and let his arms fall to his sides. "Say what's on your mind, Mark."

51

"I think you're forgetting the main victim in this case," said Jordan, still looking out the window. "It's certainly not a low-level drug dealer like Tony Mazarria. And I know Jake has a record, but it seems like a bit of a leap to go from taking co-caine to murdering somebody, especially when he's been clean for years. He just doesn't seem like the type of guy who would hurt anyone, let alone his own daughter."

"Maybe you're right," said Braxton and Jordan turned to look at him. "You know I worked narcotics in New York for a lot of years; maybe I'm letting some of that bleed over." He paused and then looked down and addressed his shoes. "Thanks for calling me out on it. I think I need that some-times."

"Maybe that's why the captain put us together," said Jordan. He cleared his throat before the silence got too awkward. "So where do we stand? Are we in agreement that Jake didn't kill Tony?"

Braxton hesitated but said, "Yes. He didn't kill him."

"Which means somebody's trying to frame Tony for killing Anne and Jake for killing Tony. Personally my bet's on Grif-fin."

"He did look a little shell-shocked when I mentioned To-ny's name. And his attitude seemed a bit...extreme. All the anger was a bit more than the situation warranted."

"You'd think he'd want to do anything in his power to help us if he really cared that his sister was dead," Jordan pointed out. "That's the attitude Jake seems to have at any rate."

Braxton sighed again and then said, "I guess the only thing left to do is apologize to Jake for accusing him of murder."

"I'll let you take the lead on that."

Braxton gave him a look that was half scowl and half smile, then reached for the door handle. They headed back into the room where Jake was still waiting quietly. His head jerked up as the door opened. He didn't even give them a chance to sit down before he started talking.

"I need you both to understand that I did not do this. I know I used to be an addict and I know I had a previous connection with Tony, but that part of my life is over. I'm a different person now; I have been ever since I got out of rehab. I would never kill anyone, and I'll do anything I have to do to prove it to you."

"Actually, you don't have to do anything to prove it," said Braxton, looking very serious. Jordan saw a look of cautious optimism dawning on Jake's face. "I was completely out of line when I accused you of murder. It's not something I should have said lightly, and I apologize."

A bit stiff, thought Jordan, smiling to himself a little. *He's not used to admitting he's wrong about something.*

"Thank you," said Jake. There was a moment of heavy silence and then Jake said, "Is there anything else I can help you with? Because if there's not, I'd like to get home. It's been a hell of a day."

"Just one thing," Jordan said. "Is there any chance—any at all—that Anne was involved with drugs? It might help us find a motive if she was."

"I don't think so. I guess I can't know for sure because I haven't been in contact with her for so long. But she saw what it was doing to me and I can't believe she would have willingly put herself into that situation." He looked Detective Jordan full in the face as he said it, and the conviction in his voice was strong.

"Well, I think that's all we have for now," said Braxton, drumming his hands along the table and standing up. The other two men followed his example. "My partner here will walk you out. Again, please call us if you think of anything."

"Absolutely," said Jake, shaking hands with both of them. Jordan led the way out of the interview room, downstairs and out of the building.

CHAPTER 10

J ake knew something was wrong the moment he pulled into his driveway. The front door was wide open and all the lights were on. He could see papers scattered across the floor, shifting slightly in the breeze.

I don't know how much more I can handle in one day, he thought. Still, the situation was not going to go away, so there was nothing else to do but deal with it. Jake vaguely remembered learning somewhere that if you came home to a burglarized house, there were three golden rules to follow: call the police, get out of the house immediately, and don't touch anything.

God, I wish I could afford a cell phone. Since he couldn't, Jake got out of his car, dashed over to his neighbor Noreen's house and began to knock on her door urgently. He had begun to fear she wasn't home and was about to leave and try someone else when he heard approaching footsteps.

"Oh hello, Jacob," she said. Her smile faded when she saw the urgency in his face. "What's wrong? Are you all right?"

"Yes, I'm fine," Jake said, thinking it was the biggest lie he'd ever told. "Listen, can I use your phone to call the police? Somebody broke into my house."

"Oh, you poor dear," said Noreen. "Come in."

"Thank you," said Jake, following her down the short hallway into her kitchen.

"Do excuse the mess," said Noreen as she handed over the phone.

Jake wondered what she meant by mess; all he saw was an open newspaper and some mail spread out on the table. Then, shaking off the thought, he pulled Detective Jordan's business card out of his pocket and dialed the number. As before, Jordan answered on the first ring.

"Detective Jordan speaking."

"Hello, detective, this is Jake Henderson." He laughed slightly then added, "I imagine you're tired of hearing from me today."

"What's wrong, Jake?" Jordan suddenly sounded much more alert. Braxton had been sitting on the edge of his desk staring vaguely into space; at the change in his partner's voice he frowned and stared down at him curiously.

"My house got broken into."

"What was missing?"

"I don't know, I didn't go inside. But the front door was wide open and there's a bunch of papers scattered all over my entryway."

"OK, where are you now?"

"Next door at my neighbor's house."

"Stay put until we get there."

"Yes, sir."

Jordan hung up and then grabbed the coat hanging from the back of his chair.

"That was Jake. He said his house has been broken into."

Braxton swore under his breath and then pulled on his own jacket.

"Yeah, my thoughts exactly," said Jordan. Both men armed themselves and were just about to leave when the receptionist stopped them.

She gestured to a man standing in front of the desk and said, "This is Karl Laytham. He said he got a call from the captain earlier?"

The man before them was tall with dark brown hair and green eyes. He wore a black leather jacket unzipped to reveal the red sweater he was wearing underneath.

"I was told to speak to either Detective Jordan or Detective Braxton," he said.

Braxton turned to his partner and said, "You go handle the robbery; Jake likes you better. I'll join you as soon as I can."

Jordan nodded briskly and left.

"Looks like I came at a bad time," said Karl, shaking hands with Detective Braxton.

"Don't worry about it. Right this way, please."

"What's this all about?" said Karl, sinking slowly down into a chair.

"I'm sorry to be the one to tell you this but—" Braxton paused and took a deep breath before delivering the bad news. "Anne was killed last night."

"Killed? Why? By who?" Karl's breathing had sped up and he seemed oblivious to the fact that his voice had taken on a nasal quality and there were tears leaking from the corners of his eyes. It was the truest expression of grief that Detective Braxton had seen thus far in this murder investigation.

"We don't know why or who," said Braxton with a sigh. "Right now we're just trying to cover all the angles."

Understanding dawned on Karl's face. "And I'm one of those angles."

"I'll be perfectly honest with you," said Braxton, leaning forward over the table not to intimidate but to show his sincerity. "I don't think you did it."

"Well that's good, because I didn't. So why am I here?" Karl's voice broke a little and he passed a hand over his eyes.

"I understand you and Anne were in a relationship?"

"Yes. We were until about a week ago."

"What was the uh…nature…of the parting?" said Braxton, wincing inwardly at his own awkward phrasing. But Karl understood what he was trying to say.

"It was a mutual agreement. She was going to start shooting a movie down in New York and we thought a long-distance relationship might be tricky."

Braxton frowned. "But wouldn't you be seeing quite a lot of her on the set?"

"I don't understand," said Karl, also frowning.

"It was my impression that you were one of the camera operators. That you helped get her the job."

"She got that job without any help from me," Karl said with a brief laugh. "I'm a bartender, not a cameraman."

"And I take it she wasn't planning on staying with you while she filmed the movie?" Braxton asked, frustration building up inside of him. *We've been focusing our investigation on the wrong person.*

"No. The movie was being shot in New York City, I live in Glenville, it's just on this side of the border between New York and Connecticut." He frowned and added, "I don't know who's been telling you all of this stuff about me but they sure don't have their facts straight."

"One more question," said Braxton. "Is there any chance Anne could have been involved with drugs?"

"Absolutely not."

"You seem pretty certain."

"Because I am. I'm sponsoring someone who's in NA so I know how recovering addicts act. Besides, Anne told me that she had watched drugs destroy the life of someone she loved. She said there was no way she would let herself get caught up in that stuff."

"You've been extremely helpful, Karl," said Braxton, standing up and opening the door. He pulled out a business card and handed it over, saying, "Please let me know if you think of anything else."

"Likewise," said Karl.

The two men left the building together and went their separate ways once they reached the parking lot.

CHAPTER 11

While his partner was speaking with Karl, Detective Jordan pulled up outside of Jake's house. On his way over he had called the officer in charge of patrolling this area, Sarah Peterson, and asked if she could meet him here. He was pleased to see that she had arrived before him. He checked his weapon and got out of the car.

Officer Peterson met him on the driveway and said, "I haven't seen anyone leave since I got here."

Looking down at the ground, Detective Jordan only saw one set of footprints; these led from Jake's car and across the yard to the house next door.

"Either the burglar is still in there or he left by the backyard," he said, mostly to himself. Then he turned to Sarah and added, "Stay close."

She nodded and followed him up the front porch steps and through the open door. It didn't take them long to clear all the rooms. Through the back door, which was standing ajar, Jordan could see a trail of footprints leading to the fence.

"Looks like that's how he got out," said Officer Peterson, making Jordan jump; he hadn't heard her approach. She laughed a little at his reaction and said, "Sorry. Didn't mean to startle you."

"I got three hours of sleep last night, I've been to two murder scenes in the past two days, and we're nowhere close to finding the killer. Sorry if my nerves are a little shot right now."

"What can I do to help?"

"Go next door and find Jake Henderson, he's the owner of the house. We need him to come and see if anything's missing. Oh, and call the forensics unit and get them to send someone over here. Maybe we'll get lucky and find something."

"Henderson...That's the last name of the girl who was murdered last night. You think this might be somehow connected?"

"I won't know unless any odd fingerprints turn up."

Officer Peterson took the hint and left. Jordan remained standing in the living room, staring out the window and thinking.

All over the house, in every room it had been the same: drawers pulled out, the contents tossed carelessly about the room. Jordan also noted that the disorder was worse in the bedrooms, which were toward the back of the house; it seemed like the thief had become more and more desperate the longer he (or she) searched.

"Someone was looking for something," Jordan murmured.

"Sorry?" said Officer Peterson; she had just returned with Jake Henderson in tow. Again, Jordan was startled at the stealth of her approach. Or maybe it was the fact that his nerves felt like high-tension wires at the moment.

"I said it seems like somebody was looking for something."

"You mean, something specific," said Jake. "So this wasn't some random burglary."

"I don't think so. But that's just my gut instinct." He turned to Officer Peterson and said, "Go outside and wait for forensics to get here. Jake and I are going to take a walk through the house and see if we can determine what was taken."

Officer Peterson left and Jake began to walk slowly through his house. It now felt like a house that belonged to someone else.

This didn't happen to me, Jake thought. *It happened to somebody else entirely. It's just a chapter in somebody else's life.* He knew this wasn't true of course, but it was the only way he felt he could handle the situation.

"Did you keep anything of value in the house?" Jordan asked. He spoke in a low voice, as if he was reluctant to interrupt Jake's private thoughts.

"I work at a power plant; I don't really have much in the way of valuables. Wait," he said. He stopped in the middle of the hallway and spun around to face Detective Jordan. "The safe."

"What safe? And more importantly, where is it?"

"On the top shelf in my closet," Jake said and rushed into his bedroom, the detective right on his heels. They both saw that the safe was still on the top shelf but there was a chair in the opening to the closet. Jake rushed forward, meaning to jump on the chair himself and pull the safe down but Detective Jordan grabbed his arm.

"What?" Jake demanded, pulling free of Detective Jordan's grip.

"If you're going to do that, wear these." He pulled a pair of latex gloves from his pocket and handed them over. Jake took them and then took the safe from the shelf and carried it to his bed, noting as he did so how light it felt.

All that was inside was the deed to the house. The color drained from Jake's face as he looked up at Detective Jordan, who had been watching from just inside the doorway.

"What is it?" said the detective, taking a step toward him; the man looked like he was about to faint. "What's wrong, what's missing?"

"When my wife and I first got married, I bought a gun to use for protection. I kept it in the safe, but it's not there now. I was licensed to carry it and I kept the permit in here but now that's gone, too."

"We'll get a copy of your permit, don't worry about that. Was the gun loaded?"

Jake shook his head. "No. But the box of ammo is also missing."

Just then, the crime scene techs walked in with their cameras and fingerprint kits.

"Move the safe back to where it was in the closet," Jordan ordered. Jake obeyed, and then the two of them left the house to get out of the way.

"This may take them a while," Jordan said. "Do you have anywhere you could stay for the night?"

"I'll just get a hotel room or something. I mean I would try to call my son, but I don't even know his number."

Jordan took out a notebook and flipped through it until he found the page where he had written down Griffin's contact information. He dialed the number on his phone and then handed it to Jake.

"Call him." Jake hesitated and then took the phone. There was no answer so Jake left a message, explaining the situation. At a nod from Detective Jordan, Jake told Griffin to call him back at that number. When Jake tried to call Griffin's cell number it went straight to voicemail. As Jake handed the phone back over it buzzed in his hand. He looked down thinking it might be Griffin calling back but it was Detective Braxton. He showed it to Jordan, who took the call.

"Hello, Steve," he said. "What's the latest?"

"Griffin's lying though his teeth, that's the latest."

"How do you know?" asked Jordan, taking a few steps away from Jake so he wouldn't overhear Braxton's side of the conversation.

"Because almost everything he told us about Karl is a lie. He's not a cameraman, he doesn't live in New York, and the decision to break up was mutual."

Jordan took a few steps farther away from Jake and said, "He also doesn't appear to be answering his home phone or his cell phone."

"Very suspicious if you ask me," said Braxton after a brief pause. "Was there anything missing from the house?"

"So far it looks like just three things, but you're not going to like what they are."

"Lay it on me."

"Jake's gun, his license to carry and a box of ammunition."

"Well, I'd say this case is turning into a nightmare. I'll be there in three minutes. Don't tell Jake about this conversation until I get there."

"You got it. See you soon."

CHAPTER 12

When Detective Braxton pulled up outside the house he went inside to speak to the forensics team. Then he came back outside and asked Detective Jordan for a private word. They left Jake standing on the porch, staring down at the boards under his feet and still wondering how all of this could happen to anybody, let alone him. He couldn't remember a time when he had felt so powerless, like he had no control over anything happening around him anymore.

The conversation between the two detectives was extremely brief. Then they came back and Detective Braxton said gently, "Are you feeling up to a few more questions, Jake?"

"What's a few more?" Jake said with a sarcastic, humorless bark of laughter. "Sorry. What do you want to know?"

"The forensics team said the door showed no signs of forced entry," said Braxton, "so it's likely that whoever did this had a key. Anybody have one apart from you?"

Jake thought for a minute then reluctantly admitted, "Griffin might have had a set." He had been looking at the ground while he spoke but he looked up in time to see a significant glance pass between the two detectives.

"What do you mean he might have had a set?" Detective Jordan asked.

"He lived in this house while he was growing up, and I know he took his keys with him when he left. But I also wouldn't be surprised if he had thrown them out; this house held a lot of bad memories for him."

"Well if he did throw them out, anyone could have picked them up," said Detective Braxton with a sigh of frustration. "And that means we'll have lost the only suspect we had."

It took a few seconds for Jake's tired mind to process Braxton's words.

"You think my son did this?" he asked in disbelief, actually staggering backwards a few steps. "No. He can't have! I mean I know he and I have had our share of differences in the past, but he's not a criminal."

Braxton and Jordan seemed to be having a telepathic conversation with their eyes. Then Jordan looked away and Braxton said, "Actually, Jake...now I know this is difficult to hear...but we have reason to believe he might be."

"What reasons?" Jake said. His voice was harsh.

"I just spoke with Karl, Anne's ex-boyfriend," Braxton said. Almost everything Griffin told us about him was a lie. And before you even ask, yes, I'm sure."

"You'll also recall the murder of Tony Mazarria this afternoon? We think he may have been responsible for that as well," Jordan said.

"I thought I committed that one," Jake lashed back at them.

"The new evidence we've obtained about Griffin's character suggests that he might have framed you," said Braxton.

"And why would he do that?"

There was a loaded silence that hung over the three of them. It was clear that this was the one question Braxton and Jordan had hoped to avoid as long as possible.

"To cover his own actions," Braxton said finally.

"Your daughter's phone was found in Mazarria's pocket. The only person who would have her phone would be the killer."

"Well maybe...maybe someone mugged her and stole her phone." Jake knew he was grasping at straws but what else could he do? He couldn't just sit back and accept that his son was a murderer.

Neither of the detectives said anything and Jake turned away, staring out across the street and seeing nothing.

"He and Anne were so close growing up. I can't imagine something happening between them that would make him angry enough to kill her."

"We're hoping he might be able to give us some answers about that. Our captain is sending two officers over to his apartment right now," said Braxton.

"They're going to arrest him?" Jake asked; that made it seem like the case was already closed.

"At this point we have no choice," Detective Jordan said. "All the evidence points to him, and now to make things worse he's armed."

"You think he's planning to attack someone else?" Jake guessed as the truth hit him.

Braxton dodged around the question and asked, "Jake, you need to find a safe place to stay until we sort this all out."

"So you think he wants to kill me." Jake was surprised by how little fear he felt at that idea; he couldn't help but think that maybe death would be a convenient way out of all the pain he was feeling. He stuck his hands in his pockets and paced back and forth on the small porch.

"My buddy Mike Levee was my sponsor while I was going through recovery," Jake said at last. "He'd probably let me crash at his place. Can I borrow your phone to give him a call?"

Jordan pulled out his phone and made to hand it over but it rang before he could.

He flipped it open and said, "Jordan speaking...Are you sure?...Well that's not entirely unexpected I guess...Put a BOLO out on his car, then canvass the area, see if you can get any leads. Steve and I will be over there shortly...Thanks, bye."

"So where will you and I be going shortly?" Detective Braxton asked. His tone was casual but his eyes were focused.

"To Griffin's apartment," Jordan answered his partner. Then he turned to Jake and added, "Your son is on the run."

CHAPTER 13

"Maybe he's not," Jake said after he'd recovered from hearing this news. "Maybe he just ran out on an errand, or went to get a bite to eat."

But Detective Jordan was shaking his head.

"When Griffin didn't come to the door, the officers went and spoke to the landlord. The man told them that Griffin had left the building ten minutes prior to their arrival, carrying a bulging duffel bag. Before he left he handed over his keys and the month's rent and said he wanted an immediate termination on his lease."

Faced with all these facts, it was no longer possible for Jake to deny that Griffin was guilty of at least something, even if it wasn't murder.

"So...now what?" he asked. "How do we go about finding him?"

"We?" Braxton repeated, frowning at Jake.

"He probably has my weapon, and you seem to think he might have killed two people already. I don't want anyone else

72

to get hurt, so I want to help you find him. Besides, he owes me some answers."

Even as Jake said this he wondered how he would phrase the question he most wanted an answer to: *Did you kill your sister, Griffin?*

"Jake, would you excuse us for a moment please?" Braxton asked. Without waiting for an answer he beckoned to his partner and they withdrew inside the house.

"Do you think we screwed up bringing Griffin in to talk earlier today?" Jordan asked him.

"You mean do I think *I* screwed up when I asked Griffin that leading question about Tony, right?" Braxton said.

"I mean what I said. We're partners, we take the blame and the victory together."

"I think it was only a matter of time before he committed another crime," Braxton said after a moment's silence. "But I think I may have just given him a little nudge."

"Well there's nothing we can do about it now," said Jordan. Privately he agreed with his partner that interrogating Griffin was the wrong move; but Braxton really didn't need to hear that. And besides, they had just been following their captain's orders. "The way I see it, the next step is simple: Griffin's on the run, we have to go and find him."

"There's still something that doesn't seem to ring true about that," Braxton said. "There's just something a little…unsettling about Griffin deciding to hit the road."

"What do you mean 'unsettling'? Seems like a confession of guilt to me. If anything, the fact that he killed his own sister and now wants to kill his father is what's unsettling."

"But what if we're looking at this the wrong way?" Braxton argued. "What if instead, we're looking at a case where a *father* murdered his daughter and now wants to frame his son for it?"

"Not this crap again!" Jordan exclaimed, giving his partner an exasperated look. "I was under the impression that it was Griffin who was on the run, not Jake."

"Maybe Griffin's just trying to protect himself."

"Exactly. He's trying to stop himself getting arrested."

"No, I mean maybe he's running away from his father."

"So Jake robbed his own house then?"

"Or this house robbery is just a completely unrelated incident."

"It's not unconnected, sir," said Sarah Peterson, joining the two detectives in the front hallway.

"What do you mean?" Both Jordan and Braxton asked the question at the same time but with completely different tones of voice. Jordan's was hopeful while his partner's demanded proof.

"Forensics dusted the safe for prints. We found Griffin's on both the inside and the outside."

"Maybe they were from years ago, when he lived here growing up," Braxton suggested, but it was with the air of a man who knows he is fighting a losing battle.

"Sorry. Prints decay over time and these were fresh."

"Are you finally going to believe Jake now?" Jordan asked.

"Yes. I believe him. I think we should focus our efforts on trying to find Griffin."

"Great idea," Jordan said under his breath as he followed his partner back outside. "Thanks, Sarah," he added over his shoulder.

"So. Jake," Braxton said without any preamble. "Do you have any idea where your son might go if he was feeling threatened?"

Jake had been thinking about this while the detectives were inside so he had his answer ready.

"I can think of two places. The first would be Anne's apartment. They were pretty close so I wouldn't be surprised if he had a key. And he probably would assume that it's the last place anybody would think to look for him."

"Makes sense," Braxton said, nodding his head slowly as he thought it over. "I'll go arrange to have it checked out." And he left to go back inside and speak with the officers there.

"You mentioned another place?" Jordan prompted.

"Griffin was very close with Mike Levee's son. They were about the same age and they saw quite a bit of each other while Mike was...you know...helping me out with stuff."

"Does Mr. Levee's son live in the area?"

"Yes. I don't know the exact address or anything but I know it was somewhere close by. And it seems likely that he and Griffin would have kept in touch."

"And his name?"

"Alex Levee."

"I'm going to call my captain and fill him in; I need his advice about what to do next. I won't be long."

Jordan pulled out his phone and walked down toward his car. Jake was left to stand on the porch alone, frustrated and to some extent fascinated by all the procedures and rules that had to be followed. He felt like some of those rules could be relaxed; didn't everyone keep saying that this was an urgent case? And now he was forced to wait while things were arranged and people were updated.

Jordan and Braxton both came back at the same time.

"I'm going to take an officer with me and go to Anne's apartment," Braxton said. "You're going to go with Detective Jordan to the power plant to have a word with Mr. Levee about his son."

"He won't be there," Jake said. "Mike got off work about three hours ago, he'd be at home."

"Then we'll go there," Jordan said without missing a beat. "A few officers will also be following us. Just in case."

"In case of what, exactly?"

Jordan took a deep breath and Jake unconsciously braced himself for bad news. "We need to consider the possibility that you are the main target. But not in the way you might think."

"All this sideways talking and beating around the bush is getting really old," Said Jake, rubbing his eyes which stung and itched from grief and tiredness.

'We don't mean—" Braxton began but Jake cut him off.

"I'm sure you don't. I'm sure you're just trying to protect me, soften whatever blow you're about to deal. But I assure you I can handle it. Whatever it is, just give it to me straight."

He glared at the pair of them; they both looked solemnly back at him and then nodded.

"OK," said Jake. "Thank you. Now I thought we had already established that my son is after me."

His detached tone of voice took even him by surprise.

"He is after you," Braxton said, still choosing his words carefully. "But we've revised our earlier opinion that he would try and kill you directly. If he wanted to do that, then why not just wait inside your home until you got back and kill you then? We think he wants to cause you as much pain as possible by killing all the people you care about."

Jake was silent. He almost regretted his request for the detectives to speak plainly to him. What they were suggesting was sick and sadistic, and yet in a twisted way it made sense. If Jake had had to go through the loss of a parent alone, at Griffin's age...and then to watch his surviving parent descend into drugs and alcohol...Yes, looking back on it made Jake shocked and disgusted at the man he had been back then and the way he had treated his children. He had hurt Griffin beyond belief, and Griffin had had a long time to dwell on that. But was he really capable of taking his hatred, his desire for revenge that far? Did he really not care how many people he killed as long as their deaths caused his father pain?

"So the officers that are coming with us aren't actually there to protect me," he said finally. "They'll be there in case he tries to come after Mike."

"Exactly," said Jordan. "He'll have at least two undercover officers watching his house around the clock until we get the whole matter straightened out. We'll do the same for Levee's son once we find him. Is there anyone else you can think of that he would go after to try and hurt you?"

Jake thought about it and then shook his head. "Mike and his family are pretty much the closest friends I have. Well..." Jake hesitated.

"What?" Braxton prompted. "Remember, Jake, even if you think it's irrelevant the smallest detail could be crucial to solving this case."

"My father lives just across the state line in New York. But I don't think Griffin would try and kill him. He was like a substitute father when I was going though all my stuff."

"Would he go there to seek asylum?" Braxton asked.

"No," Jake said definitively. "My dad would ask too many questions."

"Hmmm...he should still be given protection just in case, in my professional opinion," said Braxton. He pulled out his notebook and pencil. "What's your father's address?"

Jake gave it to them and then added, "Don't tell him what you're doing though. Just do it in secret. Is that allowed?"

"It is," said Braxton. "But why?"

"Like I said, he asks a lot of questions," Jake replied. "And he absolutely adored both of his grandchildren, but Anne especially. I know he'll find out that she's dead eventually, but it just feels like that news should come from me. And I don't know how to tell him that it was probably his grandson who did it."

"All right, Jake. We'll do it in secret; you have our word on that," Braxton assured him. "Now what about your wife's parents? Would he go to them?"

"No. They never wanted much to do with us. They hated me for being poor and they thought I purposely got their daughter pregnant in order to force her into marrying me. Then I could get my hands on their money after they died. Oh, and after that happened it only made sense that I would skip out on Margie and leave her to raise the kid."

There was a slightly stunned silence from both detectives. Jake was aware that he had probably given them too much information but he couldn't help himself. Finally revealing all these things that he had held in for years helped to relieve some of the pressure weighing on his heart.

"I wouldn't relish the family reunions," said Jordan. Something about the dry, matter-of-fact way he said it made Jake laugh, his first real laugh in quite a while. He could feel more mirth building up inside him but bit his tongue to hold it in; he didn't want the detectives to think he was insane.

"On that note, I think we should go," said Braxton, bringing the situation back to seriousness once more; he had not cracked so much as a half smile at his partner's little joke. "Time is of the essence after all."

"Quite so," Jordan agreed, all traces of humor gone. "Come on, Jake. Steve, stay in touch. And good luck."

"Same to you. I'll expect contact in an hour unless something happens before then."

CHAPTER 14

Jake walked automatically towards the cruiser that they had ridden in that morning, but Detective Jordan led him instead to an unremarkable green sedan.

"Unmarked car," he told Jake as they got in.

That explained the nondescript nature; if Jake had just seen this car driving along the street he would have no inkling that a police officer was behind the wheel. But the inside was a different story. Attached to the center console where the cup holders were, there was a computer screen on a rotating platform that could be swiveled to face either the driver or the passenger. Jake also noticed a set of hinges that would allow the screen to fold down into the center console, rendering it virtually invisible unless you already knew it was there. The keyboard was on its own swiveling platform, with hinges that would fold it into the glove compartment.

Jake pushed the keyboard gently out of the way as he slid into his seat and watched Detective Jordan messing with a radio that had far more buttons and knobs than normal.

"Just finding the proper frequency to keep in touch with the other cars," he explained to Jake. "I hate it when someone else drives," he added to himself. He stopped fiddling with the radio and started adjusting the mirrors and the seat position. Glancing over his shoulder, Jake saw the officers who would be following them making the same sort of adjustments in their car. At last, a voice crackled over the radio, making Jake jump in spite of himself.

"Ready when you are, Mark."

Jordan turned the volume down and picked up the walkie-talkie that was attached to the center console.

"We're all set up here. Just stay on our tail. And keep your eyes open."

"Copy that."

And so at last they sped on their way, with Jake playing the part of navigator. Mark lived about ten minutes away from Jake's house but they got there in half that time. It was only after they arrived that Jake realized he was gripping the sides of his seat very tightly with both hands. At first Jordan laughed but then his face grew more concerned.

"You don't get carsick, do you?"

Jake shook his head mutely, although he did feel a bit queasy. He unbuckled his seatbelt and clambered out of the car. Detective Jordan followed suit and they proceeded up the driveway towards the front porch. The two officers who had followed them over parked across the street to wait, looking entirely unobtrusive.

"I'll let you do most of the talking, since Mike knows you," Jordan said and he dropped back a few paces. When Jake rang the doorbell there was an immediate sound of barking from inside. Someone yelled, "Cooper, hush!" and then the door was opened by a small girl with curly black hair and huge brown eyes. She opened the door only a crack, but they could see Cooper, the Levees' German Shepherd standing right behind her, his nose almost touching the small of her back.

"Hi, Maria," said Jake, squatting down to her level. "Do you remember me?"

"You're Grandpa's friend, right?" the little girl asked, after thinking for a minute.

"That's right! Is Grandpa home now?"

"Yes. Would you like to see him?"

"I would like to see him. Could you go get him for me?"

"Okay," the girl said and then closed the door in Jake's face. Jake straightened up as he and Detective Jordan listened to the faint sound of her small bare feet running up the stairs. A minute later a much heavier tread was heard from inside and the door was opened again, this time by Mike Levee.

"Maria, what happened to your manners? Why did you leave our guests standing outside in the cold?"

"You told me not to let strangers in, Grandpa," Maria told him, as though it was the most obvious thing in the world. "And I didn't know who his friend was so that makes him a stranger."

"Oh, OK sweetheart," said Mike, laughing a little. "You can come on in, both of you." He stepped aside and both of them entered happily into the cozy warmth. Cooper gave a soft bark when he saw Detective Jordan but then sniffed his shoes and seemed to decide he was all right.

"Maria, why don't you go upstairs and get ready for bed? I'll come tuck you in once I'm done talking with Mr. Henderson and his friend."

"Okay," Maria agreed and dashed off back upstairs.

"Gary told me about what happened, Jake. You have my condolences. If there's anything that me and my wife can do for you..."

"Thank you," said Jake, shaking Mike's hand. "This is Detective Jordan, he's investigating what happened."

"Nice to meet you, Detective," said Mike.

"Call me Mark, please."

"And call me Mike. Now, what can I do for you?"

"I don't really know how to put this," Jake said; suddenly he found it much easier to address his shoes. He scratched Cooper behind the ears just for something to do with his hands.

"Why don't we go and sit down?" Mike suggested, gesturing toward the living room.

Mark and Jake gratefully accepted and fell into chairs on opposite sides of a crackling fire. Jake stared into it for a minute, thinking about how to say what he needed to say.

"Can you tell us how to get in touch with your son?"

"Alex? Sure. Does he have something to do with Anne's death?"

"Not exactly." Jake took a breath to steel his nerves but Detective Jordan took over.

"The police have reason to believe that Mr. Henderson's son Griffin is responsible for Anne's death."

"Griffin kill his own sister? No, no way. That's completely sick! How could you even think such a thing?"

"They have physical evidence against him, Mike," said Jake. "And I believe them. You don't know how much it kills me to say that but it's the truth."

"God, Jake," Mike said, leaning back in his chair and staring at his friend. "I don't even know what to say, man." He paused, waiting for Jake to say something. When he remained silent Mike went on, "I still don't understand what Alex has to do with all of this."

"He and Griffin kept in touch, right?" Mike nodded and Jake continued, "Griffin's on the run. We think he might have gone to Alex looking for a safe place to stay."

"Alex and his wife went out of town for their anniversary. That's why we're keeping Maria."

"We'll still need to know Alex's address so we can keep an eye on his place."

Mike rattled it off and Detective Jordan stepped into the kitchen to call some more officers.

"Hopefully they'll catch him if he does go to Alex's place," said Mike. Then he seemed to realize what he had said and looked up in horror. "Oh my God, what's wrong with me? How could I say something like that about your son? I'm sorry, I just meant...I...um..."

"I hope they catch him, too," said Jake. "Before anyone else gets hurt."

Mike studied him with narrowed eyes. "There's more to the story isn't there? Something you haven't told me yet."

"The police also think...I'm not sure if I believe them yet but they think that Griffin might actually be trying to hurt me. But not directly—they think he wants to do it by killing the people that I'm closest to."

Mike's face went pale. "And that includes me, I would imagine?"

"Yes," Jake said. "But like I said, I still have a hard time believing that Griffin would go that far."

"But we believe it," said Detective Jordan, who had reentered the room unnoticed by either of them. "There are two police officers watching your house right now from an undercover car parked across the street. The protective detail will continue until the case is solved."

"Alex and Marissa are due back home tomorrow morning. What happens if they go home and he's there?"

Jordan thought for a minute and then said, "Give them a call. I'll speak to them and explain the situation."

Mike picked up the phone but before he dialed the first digit it started ringing.

"It's Griffin," he said, staring at it. He looked up at Detective Jordan, plainly terrified. "What should I do?"

"This is very important, Mike," said Detective Jordan, doing some quick thinking. "You're going to put it on speakerphone and answer it. Act like nothing's wrong, act totally natural. Can you do that?"

Mike still looked scared but when he answered the phone, his voice was natural enough. "Hello?"

"Hi, Mr. Levee. This is Griffin Henderson. I don't know if you remember me or not, but you were my father's sponsor for drug rehab?"

Jake could hear that Griffin was trying to keep his tone conversational, but he could also hear the anger lurking just behind it. It took all he had not to say something but he held his tongue at a warning look from the detective standing beside him.

"Sure I remember you, Griffin. Haven't heard from you in ages."

"Yeah. Sorry to call out of the blue like this. I just wanted to ask you something."

"Of course. What's on your mind?"

"It's actually about a friend of mine. He's having the same kind of issues my dad had back when I was growing up. I want to get him some help, but I'm not exactly sure how the whole Narcotics Anonymous thing works from the point of view of a sponsor."

Detective Jordan started very quietly writing a message on his notepad. To give him time to write, Mike kept talking.

"Have you been to their website?"

"I have, and it was very helpful and all but I really just wanted to talk to someone who had experience with it first hand."

"Well what about you dad?" Mike gave Jake an apologetic glance as he spoke. "I mean don't get me wrong, I'm honored that you trust me enough to ask me about this but your dad could really give you the ins and outs of it."

Jake closed his eyes, ready to force himself to be silent, no matter how much he didn't like Griffin's response.

"My father and I have barely spoken since I left home." The lack of emotion in Griffin's voice was worse than if he had shouted in anger.

Jake didn't have long to dwell on it, though. While Griffin was still speaking, Detective Jordan passed over the note he had written: *Invite him over here to talk about it.* Mike shook his head and pointed toward the ceiling; Jake knew that at that moment his only thought was for his granddaughter. But Detective Jordan pointed first at himself and then at the unmarked car across the street, which was just visible through the living room window. His message was clear enough: *There are multiple police officers here; she'll be fine.* He tapped twice on his written message: *Just do it.*

"You still there, Mike?"

"Yeah, I'm still here," Mike said quickly, simultaneously nodding to Detective Jordan. "Phone cut out on me for a second. What were you saying?"

"I was just saying that my father and I haven't been on good terms for a long time now. I don't feel like bringing up the past would be a good way to reopen lines of communication, even if I wanted to."

"I guess I can understand that. Listen, why don't you come over? That way we can talk about all your questions."

Griffin hesitated. Jake assumed he was just thinking the offer over but beside him Detective Jordan's eyes narrowed. He heard suspicion in that silence, or so it seemed to him. Had Griffin somehow guessed that a trap was being laid?

"It's too late for me to come over tonight," he said finally. "I wouldn't want to intrude, and besides I pulled the early shift at work tomorrow." Detective Jordan's eyes were now almost invisible, his brow was furrowed so deeply. Griffin continued speaking, "Why don't we meet for lunch? There's a restaurant down by the fishing piers, I can't remember the name…they have great seafood, though. It's in a big glass building across from the art museum."

"Ah, I know which one you're talking about," said Mike as Detective Jordan started writing another message. "Isn't it called Jack's Fishery?"

"Yeah, that's the one. So what do you say? Would around noon work for you?"

Right on cue, Jordan showed Mike the new message: *Say yes.*

"That would work just fine. I guess I'll see you then."

"Sounds good. Oh," he added, "Just one more thing. Do you know if Alex got a new phone number recently or something? I tried the number I have and it said it had been disconnected."

Mike gave Griffin Alex's number and then asked, "You don't need him for anything urgent, do you? Because he and his wife are out of town for a few days. I could give you their number at the hotel if you want."

"No, it's nothing important. He just wanted to buy one of my old guitars and I was going to talk price with him."

"Oh all right. Well, I hope you get in touch with him. See you tomorrow."

"Thanks, Mr. Levee. Bye for now."

He hung up and the three men in the room let out a collective breath they hadn't realized they'd been holding until that moment.

CHAPTER 15

For a minute or two there was silence except for the soft squeaking of Detective Jordan's shoes as he paced back and forth. Each man was lost in his own thoughts.

Jordan was thinking about the next step, which would be to have Mike meet with Griffin. They had plenty of time to plan, and they could easily arrange to have undercover officers stationed nearby. After all, the main concern was for Mike's safety. But another big worry Jordan had was whether or not Mike had the gall to actually go through with this and pull off a convincing performance.

Mike Levee was thinking along the same lines as Detective Jordan. Was he actually capable of sitting down to lunch with Griffin and acting completely natural when he knew there was a distinct possibility that he was eating with a murderer? The honest answer to that question was that he didn't know. What he did know was that he would just have to try his best when the time came, both for his friend's sake and to stop anyone else from getting hurt. And yet, there was still a small and selfish part of him that wished that Jake had never come to him. Mike tried not to examine this part of himself too closely, but he couldn't deny that it was there.

Jake, in addition to all the anger he felt toward his son, was now feeling guilty about involving Mike in the situation. He knew that Mike wouldn't think it was intentional—after all, Jake had only been trying to keep Mike and his family safe. But that plan had certainly backfired hadn't it? His friend was now in more danger than ever. Finally, the silence became too loud for Jake to stand.

"I'm sorry, Mike," he said abruptly. Mike, jerked out of his own thoughts, looked up at him in surprise, as if he had forgotten Jake was there. Jake was looking at him as though expecting some sort of reply, but Mike kept quiet; he could think of nothing to say. Jake let the silence spin on for a few more seconds and then continued.

"I'm so, so sorry for dragging you into all of this mess. This is my fault, all of it."

He realized even as he said it that this was the main core of everything that was weighing him down. Even worse than everything else combined—the grief and anger and confusion— was the feeling of irrational but inescapable guilt.

"I don't blame you, Jake," Mike said gently. "I know you were just trying to keep me and my family from getting hurt."

"That worked like a dream, didn't it?" Jake snorted. He ran his hands through his hair and then stood up and stared into the fireplace. "I keep feeling that things would have turned out differently if I had actually been there for my kids when they were growing up."

Mike wanted to step in and tell Jake he was being stupid, that even kids from the best families sometimes turned out badly and no one quite knew why. But he kept quiet because he could see in Jake's eyes that even though it was causing him great pain to say all of this, getting it off his chest was making him feel just a little bit better. So Mike contented himself with giving Jake his fullest attention and reserving any kind of judgment.

"If I had been a good father, Griffin wouldn't want to cause me pain by killing everyone I love, and that means I wouldn't have had to come over here in the first place, and that means you never would have been involved in some undercover police operation. I assume that's what's going to happen tomorrow?" he added to Detective Jordan. The detective, who had stopped pacing to listen to their conversation, nodded. He opened his mouth to speak but Mike Levee held up a hand to forestall him.

"Before we get into all of that," he said, "I need to say something."

"I need to make a few phone calls anyway before we discuss the next step," Detective Jordan said, taking the hint from Mike that he wanted this conversation to be private. "Excuse me for a moment." And he stepped into the kitchen, pulling out his cell phone as he went. Cooper followed behind him, hopeful that he was heading for the jar of dog treats on the counter. That left Mike and Jake alone.

"How long have we known each other, Jake?"

"Twelve, thirteen years now?"

"Exactly. Enough time for me to know that you would never intentionally put another person in danger or cause them harm. Quite the opposite, actually. You would be the guy to stick his neck out trying to help."

But Jake shook his head. "That's you, Mike. How many times did you bail me out of trouble? Persuade the boss to give me just one more chance, even though both of you knew I was a full-on junkie by that point? And I have caused people harm. Just look what I did to my own kids."

"I didn't say you had never harmed anyone," said Mike. "I said you never *intentionally* harmed anyone. If you hadn't gotten involved with drugs, would you ever have neglected Anne and Griffin?"

Jake hesitated. "Look, what does it matter? The fact is—" But Mike cut him off.

"Just answer the question, Jake. Yes or no. If you hadn't gotten involved with drugs, would you ever have neglected your children?"

"No," said Jake with a tired sigh.

"And would you ever have gotten into drugs in the first place if Margie was still here?"

Great, Mike, bring up some more painful memories, Jake thought. But at the same time, he thought he saw where Mike was going with this line of conversation.

"I can't say for sure. And now I'll never know, will I?"

"Exactly," Mike said, standing up so he could look directly into Jake's eyes as he spoke. "You don't know what would have happened if the past was different. All you can do is work with the hand you're dealt."

Jake didn't want to admit it, but what Mike was saying made a lot of sense.

"I know I can't change the past, but—"

"No buts. You're being stupid, Jake." He felt slight regret at saying these words because anger flashed across Jake's features; but at least that anger wasn't focused inward. "If you know you can't change the past, then why do you keep dwelling on it?"

Jake thought carefully before answering. He also clenched and unclenched his hands a few times so that he could speak calmly as opposed to shouting.

"I guess out of past, present and future, the past is the easiest one to think about. At least there was a little bit of good back then. Present and future, I'm alone no matter what."

"Who says you're alone? I'm here now and I'll still be here for the foreseeable future."

"You're really not mad that I got you mixed up in all of this?" Jake's voice was tentative, and Mike thought he detected a note of pleading behind it. Hearing that, especially considering who it was coming from, scared him almost as badly as having to eat lunch with someone who was the prime suspect of a murder investigation.

"No, Jake. I'm not mad."

"Thank you, Mike. I can't even express how much of a relief that is right now."

"Just think about how you'll feel tomorrow after it's all over."

It will never be over for me, Jake thought. But all he said was, "You're right. I just hope whatever scheme they come up with actually works."

"It will work," Detective Jordan assured them, coming back from the kitchen. "But we'll discuss it in the morning. Right now both of you need some rest. Mike, can you come by the police station at around 10:00 tomorrow morning? That'll give us enough time to prep you about how things are going to happen."

"I'll be there."

"Good."

"What about me?" Jake asked.

"You'll be staying home tomorrow, Jake." Detective Jordan's voice left no room for argument, but that didn't stop Jake from arguing anyway.

"Why?" he asked. "How can you expect me to just sit at home while all of this is going on, knowing my friend might be in danger?"

"He will not be in any danger," Detective Jordan snapped. His nerves were very much on edge and he was in no mood for pointless questioning. "You need to trust my partner and I to do our jobs."

"Sorry," Jake said quietly. It was clear from his tone that he truly meant it.

"I am, too," Jordan sighed; his tone was much calmer now. "I believe—and so does my captain—that you being near the restaurant would severely compromise our chances of success. If he sees you he might realize something's up."

"But he's seen you and Detective Braxton before, too. Won't that—how did you put it—'severely compromise' your chances of success?"

"The issue will be addressed, I can assure you," Jordan replied curtly. And he pressed on before Jake could argue any further. "But there are two matters of business to discuss first. Firstly, Mike, I just want to remind you that you will be safe here tonight, thanks to the protective detail across the street. I've written down a phone number for you to use if you need to get in touch with them."

"Thank you," Mike said.

"As for you, Jake, we've arranged for you to stay in a hotel, with an undercover detective in the adjoining room."

"I thought the plan was for me to stay here?" He turned to Mike and added, "That's what I was coming to ask you before things got a little off track."

"My captain doesn't think that's the best option." He went on before Jake could say anything else. "Now, unless you have any questions, Mike, I think it's time for us to be going."

After telling the detective he could think of no questions to ask, Mike walked them to the door. As Jake and Detective Jordan were leaving, a car pulled into the driveway. Jordan's hand twitched toward his weapon but Mike reached out and pushed his hand aside.

"Please don't frighten my wife," he said quietly. Detective Jordan relaxed and gave him an apologetic look.

"Is everything all right, dear?" Joann Levee asked, walking up to the door and greeting her husband with a kiss.

"Come on. I'll explain everything inside."

A worried frown creased her brow but she went in the house, and was treated to an enthusiastic greeting by Cooper.

"Good night, Jake. Detective Jordan."

"Good night, Mike. Thank you for all your help. I'll see you tomorrow morning."

Jake couldn't bring himself to say anything.

Mike watched them until they drove off; then he went inside to tell his wife about his plans for the next day.

CHAPTER 16

The hotel where Detective Jordan dropped Jake off was maybe not the nicest place, but it was still at least a place to sleep in relative comfort.

"I'll wait here with you until Clarence Sposito arrives," Detective Jordan said.

"I'm fine, really," Jake insisted. "I just want to be left alone so I can get some sleep." But Jake somehow didn't think he would be getting much sleep that night.

"Captain's orders," said Detective Jordan.

"Why's that?" Jake asked. And then before he could stop himself he added, "Your captain doesn't trust me?"

"What would make you think that?" Jordan asked, but he didn't deny it outright.

"Because right from the start of this investigation I've been treated like a criminal when I didn't do anything. I've told you time and time again, and I just don't understand why nobody will believe me."

"It's not that we don't believe you. Trust me, I don't think you did it, and neither does my captain. We just don't want to put you or any of your friends in any unnecessary danger."

"So that's why you won't let me spend the night at Mike's house. You think Griffin might try to kill two birds with one stone, so to speak. Take out me and Mike at the same time."

"Exactly. That's all it is."

Jake thought Detective Jordan wasn't being entirely truthful. If he really would be putting his friends in danger by being near them, then why had they suggested he go to Mike's house in the first place? But he didn't have time to voice his doubts because at that moment, Officer Sposito arrived. He had come from Jake's house and had with him some pajamas, a toothbrush and toothpaste, and a fresh change of clothes for the next day. It was a small gesture but it did a great deal to cheer Jake up.

Detective Jordan stood up to leave and said, "I know tomorrow's going to be rough on you, Jake and I'm sorry it has to be done this way. But you have my word that as soon as anything happens, you'll know about it."

"Thank you. That means a lot," Jake told him. He paused for a fraction of a second and then added, "And I know you know how to do your job. Sorry if that didn't come across earlier."

"Not to worry, Jake."

The two men shook hands and Jordan left. There was very little prospect of sleep for him; he was headed back to the precinct to discuss the procedure for tomorrow.

Detective Braxton pulled into the parking lot just as Jordan did.

"Heard you had an interesting night," Braxton said as a form of greeting.

"Much more interesting than I would have liked," Jordan replied, walking inside the mercifully warm lobby. "How was yours?"

"Not quite as exciting, but still productive. More evidence keeps piling up against Griffin."

"You mean evidence that's more than just circumstantial?"

They started up the stairs toward their captain's office.

"Forensics put a rush on the fingerprints from the safe; turns out they match the ones found on Anne's phone. That good enough for you?"

"It's great," Jordan said. "Unfortunately all it proves is that he had her phone; it doesn't prove that he killed her."

"No, it doesn't. But it does give us some good leverage to hold over his head when we're trying to get a confession out of him."

They proceeded upstairs and entered their captain's office.

"Sit down, both of you," their captain said as they came in. There was a steaming Styrofoam cup in front of each of their places at the desk.

It wasn't the same as a good night's sleep but it was a lot better than nothing, Jordan thought as he took his seat. He took a sip of the coffee and sighed with relief, although it tasted horrible.

"So," Captain Huntington said, "we've got a lot to discuss and I'm going to try and make this as quick as possible so you can both be well-rested when this goes down tomorrow. Either of you have any general ideas about what the plan should be?"

Braxton jumped in before Jordan had a chance to say anything.

"We could replace their waiter with an undercover officer. That way we'd be able to keep an eye and an ear on what's going on."

"I agree we need to be as close to the action as possible but I don't think we should have someone be their waiter," Jordan said, causing Braxton to glare at him. "For one thing, he would be going back and forth so it would give us a very incomplete picture of what's going on. Also, replacing the waiter would require informing the entire staff of the restaurant as to what we're doing. The more people that know about this, the more chance there is that someone slips and gives something away."

They both looked at Captain Huntington, waiting for him to cast the tie-breaking vote.

"I agree with Mark. We'll station plainclothes officers throughout the restaurant; that way we'll be better equipped to catch Griffin if he tries to make a run for it. Now, the officers closest to them will be able to tell us some of what was said but their testimony won't be much good in court. I propose having Mike Levee wear a wire while talking to Griffin."

"Bad idea, captain," Braxton said, shaking his head. "I was looking into Griffin's past and he's taken quite a few courses in criminal justice. He'd recognize a wire for sure."

"What's his job? Does it have anything to do with criminal justice?" the captain asked, frowning.

"Hardly. He works in a dry cleaner's."

"So why take classes about criminal justice and police procedure, I wonder?" the captain mused.

"Preparation for committing this crime is what it sounds like to me," Jordan said.

"Add it to the list of questions you can ask when you're interrogating him. Because we're definitely going to need a confession. That will be the strongest piece of evidence we have in this case."

"It might be the only piece of evidence," Detective Jordan said grimly, leaning back in his chair and folding his arms. "Everything we have right now is circumstantial at best. Even his fingerprints being found on her phone doesn't prove any sort of intent."

"There might be more evidence in his apartment," Braxton suggested. "Officers are going through it right now, they might get lucky. Jake's gun would certainly be nice to have."

"Or something that ties him to Tony Mazarria," Jordan added. "That way even if the evidence tying him to the death of his sister falls through we can still get him on something."

"Given the background you just described, Steve, I wouldn't get your hopes up about finding the weapon that easily. I also don't think he would risk bringing it to the restaurant tomorrow, but we still need to be prepared for that possibility. It is my opinion that we should provide Mr. Levee with a bulletproof vest—a thin one, so it doesn't show underneath his shirt. But even a thin vest will give him the protection he needs."

Both detectives indicated their agreement.

"Ideally we need to wait for Griffin to say something incriminating before we go in and arrest him," Captain Huntington said next. "But if he's too on edge and doesn't talk…is there anything else we can hold him on?"

"We can hold him for 72 hours without charging him for anything. That ought to be plenty of time to get a confession," Jordan said with confidence.

"Good. As I said, I'm depending on you two. I trust that you won't let me down."

"We won't, captain."

"All right. Now, one last thing: you'll be watching from a distance tomorrow because Griffin knows both of your faces. But you'll still be in direct contact with the undercover officers. If you spot something suspicious that they don't see, or if some new evidence from the lab comes in that ties Griffin to the burglary or to either murder, you need to inform them right away. Understood?"

"Yes, sir," they both said in unison.

"Good," said the police captain, rising from his chair. Jordan and Braxton followed suit. "Now both of you go home and get some sleep. You're in for another long day tomorrow."

* * *

The next morning, Mike Levee arrived at the police station at 10:00 as scheduled. Braxton and Jordan had already been there for almost an hour, putting finishing touches on their plan and briefing the other detectives that would be taking part in the operation.

"Ah, Mr. Levee," said Detective Jordan, having caught sight of him entering the main room. "I'd like to introduce you to my partner, Detective Steve Braxton."

"Pleased to meet you, sir," said Mike, shaking hands.

"How are you feeling this morning?" Braxton asked.

"Nervous. But I still want to do this."

"Good man," Braxton said, clapping him on the shoulder. "Just try not to show your nerves."

"Will the two of you be there in case something goes wrong?"

"Not us in particular," Jordan said. "As Jake pointed out last night, Griffin already knows our faces. But other detectives will be stationed close by."

"Jake's not usually like that, you know," Mike told him. "I hope him being argumentative last night didn't offend you or anything. He just likes feeling like he's in control, and with all of this going on…"

"Jake already apologized. And quite honestly he's far from being the worst person I've had to deal with. A woman slapped me across the face on of my first cases."

"Is that the only time that's happened?" Braxton asked, not bothering to hide his laughter.

"Yes. So far at least."

"Just wait. There'll be more."

"Well my disposition isn't quite as prickly as yours."

Braxton's only response was to give a theatrical roll of his eyes. Mike recognized that the purpose of their banter was to put him a little more at ease and he appreciated the effort. His stomach did feel a bit less squirmy.

"We'll give you all the details about what's going to happen as soon as our captain gets back. He just had to step out for a moment," Detective Jordan told Mike. "Why don't you have a seat in the meantime?" And he offered his own desk chair.

But as soon as he was going to sit down, Detective Braxton said, "Oh, here he comes now."

Mike stood up again as the captain approached them.

"Hello, Mr. Levee. My name is Captain Neil Huntington. Thank you so much for helping us out with this."

"No problem, sir. And please, call me Mike."

"All right then, Mike. Why don't I take you to my office? I just need a private word with these two, and then we'll join you."

"Okay," Mike replied. He sat down across from the captain's desk and the detectives and Captain Huntington stepped outside the door.

"What's up, captain?" Braxton asked as he closed the door to the captain's office. He couldn't interpret the look on Huntington's face.

"Well, there's good news and bad news," the captain said after taking a few moments to collect his thoughts.

"Are you going to ask us which kind we want first?" Jordan asked. The remark earned him two scowls, one from his boss and one from his partner.

"The good news is that the forensics unit found a bloody footprint in the alley where the drug dealer was killed and they think it might belong to Griffin. The bad news is that we need to find the shoes that made that print."

"And he's probably already trashed them because he knows how hard it is to get rid of blood evidence," Braxton said in a disappointed tone of voice.

"Glad you see the problem," Captain Huntington said. "They're still working on forensics from the other crime scenes."

"What about Anne's phone?"

"Techs have put a rush on it to figure out what history has been deleted; but they still haven't recovered anything pertinent, and they don't know who actually deleted all the data. They say they'll try to get back to us by the end of the day."

"Let's hope it's sooner rather than later," Jordan said.

"How about we just keep on hoping that Griffin slips up?" Braxton said.

"That's another thing I wanted to talk to you about. What if we delicately encourage him to slip up? Have Mr. Levee ask him questions about what he's been up to, how he's dealing with the loss of his sister. They would be reasonable enough things to ask and they might get Griffin to talk."

"I really don't think he'd just confess outright, especially given that Mike is Jake's best friend," said Jordan.

"Actually I think he might," Braxton said.

"What are you talking about?" Jordan asked.

"Yes, do explain, Steve," Captain Huntington added.

"I think part of him wants to get caught. His crimes are screaming for attention, the drug dealer murder especially. And he's been awfully sloppy, what with using his own key to break into his father's home and leaving fingerprints everywhere. I just feel like he would be a lot more careful if he was serious about becoming a serial killer or something."

"All killers make mistakes when they're first starting," Jordan pointed out.

"But not all killers have taken classes in forensic science and criminal justice."

"Okay, let's say you're right," said Jordan; the idea made more sense than he wanted to admit. "If that's the case, then asking Mike to lead Griffin on will only put him in more danger."

"Why don't we see what he thinks about it?" Captain Huntington suggested. Without waiting for them to reply, he led the way back into his office. Jordan noted that Mike was once again looking pale and nervous.

This is never going to work, Jordan thought.

But it has to work, another part of his mind answered. He had no choice but to trust in the abilities of a total stranger.

"I know this is going to be difficult advice to swallow, Mike," Captain Huntington said, "but try to relax. You're in very capable hands with my detectives, and I assure you our top priority is your safety. We have taken several precautions to that end."

He then launched into his spiel about the bulletproof vest, what tables the undercover officers would be sitting at, and the distress signal that Mike was to give if he thought things were getting out of hand (knocking over his drink and saying, "Here, let me clean that up.")

Mike paid very close attention to that speech, uptight and preoccupied though he was. It actually calmed him down considerably to hear all the minute details. It made him feel more in control, like he was just an actor stepping onto the stage. It was almost 10:30 by the time the police captain was finished reviewing everything.

Then he leaned back in his chair and asked, "Now, what questions do you have? Is there anything you don't understand, anything you want me to go back over?"

"I understand everything," Mike said, after clearing his throat. "It's just…"

"What's on your mind?" Captain Huntington prompted him when he hesitated.

"I just wish I knew what to say to him. I mean, knowing what I do about him makes it really hard to make small talk."

Mike glanced up from his lap in time to see all three men exchange a glance with one another.

"My advice is this," the police captain began. "Try to forget what you know, or at least try not to dwell on it. Also, let him direct the conversation as much as possible." But now it was his turn to hesitate.

"There's something else isn't there?" Mike asked.

"If you feel comfortable doing so," Huntington said, folding his hands in front of him on the desk and leaning forward, "maybe you could ask him a few particular questions: how he's been dealing with things, what he's been up to lately, things like that."

"You think he's just gonna confess to me?" Mike asked, his voice heavy with skepticism.

"We don't need him to confess outright," Braxton explained. "But if we're lucky, he might slip up, say something to incriminate himself."

"What do you mean?"

110

"Like revealing some detail of the crime that we didn't tell him about."

"Something he would only know if he was there when the crime was committed," Mike said, nodding slowly as he realized what Braxton was talking about.

"Exactly," Captain Huntington confirmed. "That would give us the probable cause we need to arrest him. If he doesn't say anything don't worry, and definitely don't push it. There's some other evidence that we're examining that should be back before too long. But I would rather make the arrest sooner than later."

"I think I agree with you on that," Mike said with an attempt at a small laugh. "The sooner he gets arrested, the sooner I can go home and try to forget this whole experience. I'll do my best to get him to slip."

"Just make sure you ask those questions casually," Jordan advised him. "We don't want to do anything to raise his suspicions."

"Understood."

"Excellent," Captain Huntington declared, sitting back and rubbing his hands together. "Are there any other matters we need to discuss?"

"I've just thought of something," Detective Jordan said, even while his partner was shaking his head.

"What is it?" Huntington demanded.

"I think Griffin might be holed up in your son's apartment, Mike. The kind of questions he was asking over the phone last night…it sounded like he was fishing for information, trying to make sure Alex's place would be a safe hideout where he could lie low."

"And I just went on and gave it to him," Mike said, angry that he hadn't been able to see what Griffin was doing.

"Don't worry about it, Mike," the captain said in a distracted sort of way. "If we could surprise Griffin while he's still there, you might not even need to go through having lunch with him. Is it your son's name on the lease?"

"Yes. Why do you ask?"

"We need his permission before we enter the residence and search it. Could you call him?"

But Mike shook his head. "He and his wife are on a plane right now headed home. It'll be after lunchtime by the time they get back."

"Ah, well. It was a nice idea," said Captain Huntington.

Mike glanced at his watch and saw that it was almost 11:00, still an hour to go until his lunch meeting.

"Sir, if there's nothing else right now, could I wait at home with my wife until the time comes for me to be at the restaurant? I think it would make her feel more comfortable. Well, it would make both of us feel more comfortable actually."

"I'm sorry, but I'm afraid we can't let you do that." The look in Captain Huntington's eyes showed that the apology was sincere.

"Why not?" he asked. He did not argue with the decision—he had enough sense to know that it would be a waste of breath—but he was still curious about the reason.

"Because you're supposed to be at work right now," Detective Braxton explained. "Let's say Griffin drives past your house. If he sees both your car and your wife's car in the driveway, that would strike him as very suspicious."

It caused a tangible pain in Mike's chest to think of his wife and Maria at home alone, with Griffin just casually driving by.

"It takes about twenty minutes to get to the restaurant from here," said Detective Jordan. "You'll wait until about half past in one of our interview rooms. Then you drive over there and we'll follow you."

"That gets me there a little early."

"That's what we want. We want tabs on him from the moment he arrives."

As Detective Jordan led Mike to a free room where he could sit and wait, Mike thought: *Thirty minutes. Just thirty minutes to change my mind and then there's no turning back.*

But as nervous as he was, he knew he wouldn't change his mind. This was something he had to do.

CHAPTER 17

The thirty minutes seemed more like thirty seconds to Mike. He spent most of the time on the phone with his wife, after obtaining the detectives' permission to call her. He could tell she was desperately worried about him, and he loved her for that. But he loved her even more because she tried to hide it and be nothing but supportive. She made him promise to call her as soon as he finished with lunch. Then she told him that since Maria wanted to celebrate the first day of her Christmas break, she thought it would be nice if they all went to the park that afternoon.

"We'll bring the sled, and maybe some mugs full of hot chocolate. And we'll all work together and build a big snowman."

"Be sure to bring a carrot for the nose," said Mike. "And my old scarf, and maybe some of the buttons from your sewing kit, too."

"You just be sure you're here to remind me. I'll never remember all these things on my own."

114

"I'll be there," Mike promised. Just then, Detective Jordan quietly opened the door and pointed at his watch. Mike nodded to him and said, "Half past eleven. I've got to go, sweetheart."

"Please be careful, dear," his wife said, and he could tell by the slightly pinched quality to her voice that she was fighting back tears. "I love you so much."

"I love you, too. Bye." Mike hung up before his wife started crying; that would have made it extremely difficult if not impossible to go through with what he was about to do.

"Ready to go?" Jordan asked him.

"Yeah. I guess I'm as ready as I'll ever be."

With that, they left the interview room and were joined by Detective Braxton on their way to the parking garage.

"Where are all the other detectives I met this morning?" Mike asked as they walked through the abnormally quiet squad room. "The ones who will be watching my back, I mean."

"They're already at the restaurant scoping things out," Braxton explained.

When they reached Mike's car, Detective Jordan placed a hand on Mike's shoulder and said, "Don't be nervous, okay? Remember, just act as natural as possible so Griffin doesn't get spooked."

"Someone will be looking out for you at all times," Braxton chimed in. "So don't worry about that aspect of it either."

"I'm fine," Mike said. Mentally he added *Every time someone tells me not to be nervous I get more and more nervous.* "I guess I'll talk to you guys after lunch."

He didn't think he could bear their concerned looks for a split second longer so he got in his car and closed the door. He fumbled with the key for a minute—his hands were shaking slightly, no matter how hard he tried to make them stop—and then started the engine. Jordan and Braxton headed to their own car, which was parked nearby. As he'd been told, Mike waited for them to start their car before driving out of the underground garage into the bright sunshine of a beautiful winter's day.

As he drove toward Jack's Fishery Restaurant, Mike blared the radio and forced himself to concentrate on each individual word in the lyrics. The method worked because by the time he got to the fishing piers where the restaurant was and pulled in the parking lot, he was actually feeling remarkably calm. Glancing in his rearview mirror, he could just make out the dark green sedan parked half a block away where he knew Braxton and Jordan were stationed.

Although they could not be in the restaurant, they would still be able to play their part; this was the only road someone could take to get here, so they would be able to call ahead to their colleagues and give them a few minutes' warning when Griffin arrived. And if he tried to make a run for it by car they could easily block him. The police captain had also explained that they would be listening in on the recording that the other detectives would be taking of the meeting. That way the moment Griffin slipped up, they could give the go-ahead to arrest him.

Mike glanced at the clock on the dashboard; it was 11:55. Whether he was ready for it or not, whether he liked it or not, it was time to get this done. He said a final quick prayer—*Lord, keep me safe and give me the right things to say*—and got out of his car. He was halfway to the front door of the restaurant when he heard a voice from behind him.

"Hey, Mr. Levee!"

It was Griffin. How long had he been sitting there waiting for Mike to arrive?

"Hello, Griffin," he said, injecting all the cheerfulness into his voice that he possibly could. "And how many times do I have to ask you to call me Mike?"

"Old habits die hard, I guess. Long time no see," Griffin said, approaching Mike and holding out his hand.

Mike took it, but he was somewhat cautious. *Could he be hiding some weapon up his sleeve?* But no harm came from the handshake.

"Same here," Mike said. "How have you been, Griffin?"

"All right I guess," Griffin replied, but the light in his eyes seemed to dim a little bit.

"Sorry," Mike said; he really meant it, too. Even with the knowledge of Griffin's criminal activities riding on his shoulders, Griffin looked so miserable in that moment that Mike really did feel for him. "That was probably a stupid thing to say, given what you've been through the past couple of days."

"How do you know what I've been through?" Griffin's voice was suddenly sharp and suspicious. Much more suspicious than the situation called for, at least in Mike's opinion. Then again, maybe that was just Griffin's defense mechanism against the grief.

"Your father called me last night, just after you did in fact," Mike told him. "He told me about Anne. I'm so sorry for your loss."

"Figures he'd call you. Can't call his son to check up on him but he'll call his friend to get some free sympathy."

Again, Mike was struck by how Griffin's emotion seemed much too extreme than the situation warranted. The level of emotion was almost—he struggled mentally to find the right word—*theatrical*. It was almost as though Griffin was a new actor who was just a bit too eager when it came to getting into his character. If he really was a murderer—Mike actually shivered at the thought—the theatrical act would certainly fit.

"You're shivering, sir," Griffin said.

"It's below freezing out here," Mike said, immensely grateful for that fact although he usually hated winter. "Why don't we go inside and warm up a bit?"

"Sure. Yeah, why not?" But he seemed distracted. Mike guessed his mind was still on his dad. They walked forward a few steps but then Griffin stopped. It took a few seconds for Mike to realize that Griffin was no longer next to him.

118

"Anything wrong?" Mike asked.

"Just something I forgot," Griffin replied. He turned as though he was going to head back to his car and looked in both directions. Some survival instinct deep within Mike gave him a bad feeling. Sure enough, Griffin suddenly pivoted and pulled his left hand out of his pocket. It was only when Mike saw the gun that he realized the bushes around the parking lot were blocking his view of the detectives' car.

That meant that they couldn't see him.

And that meant it was just him, Griffin, and a loaded gun pointed dead center at his chest.

CHAPTER 18

There goes Griffin," Braxton muttered. He had a pair of binoculars pressed to his face.

"Detective Ryan, do you read me?" Detective Jordan said into the walkie-talkie in his lap.

"Yes, thank you," said a man's voice in reply. "Everything's fine."

So the waitress must be there, Jordan thought. Out loud he said, "Griffin has just arrived. He and Mike should be entering the restaurant momentarily."

"So much for a warning."

"He must have gotten here before we did," Jordan said. "Just keep an eye out for him and get ready to start recording."

"I wonder why, though," Braxton said.

"Why what?"

"Why he got here so early."

It took a moment for what Braxton was saying to sink in.

"You think he knows this is a trap?"

"I don't know yet. But you have to admit, he is behaving rather oddly."

"If he knows it's a trap, why would he bother showing up at all?" Jordan asked. But he thought he knew what his partner's answer would be.

Sure enough, Braxton said, "Because he wants to be caught."

"Well maybe he just got the time mixed up," Jordan said, but without much conviction. Braxton actually turned in his seat to give him a cold look.

"Or maybe you made a mistake last night. You made a noise or did something to tip Griffin off that somebody else was there when he called Mike."

"I know how to do my job, Steve. Why don't you do yours and watch the parking lot?"

Braxton made no reply but raised the binoculars to his eyes once more. He watched for a few seconds then said, "They've gone behind the bushes. See if you can get them from your vantage point."

Jordan took the proffered binoculars and looked toward the restaurant parking lot.

"I can't see them either. They've probably gone inside already."

He flipped a switch on the walkie-talkie and spoke into it once more.

"Does anybody have a visual on Mike and Griffin?"

A chorus of voices answered in the negative.

The partners glanced at each other, and the same fear was in both of their faces. It was Braxton who gave voice to it.

"Something's not right."

Even as he spoke, they heard the sound of a gunshot.

Braxton immediately jammed the car into gear and they shot forward.

"All of you get outside right now!" Jordan yelled into the radio.

The next few minutes were nothing but a confused, hectic blur. In all, eight detectives had been part of the operation: three pairs stationed at various locations throughout the restaurant, plus Jordan and Braxton. By the time Braxton and Jordan got to the parking lot, two of the detectives from the restaurant were kneeling on the ground beside Mike; one was struggling to control the crowd of restaurant goers who had all started to run outside when they heard the commotion; and three were chasing after Griffin, who had a very good head start. There was no way they would be able to catch him on foot. But if someone were to block him with a car...

His partner seemed to be thinking along the same lines.

"You get control of this crime scene before it turns into a circus," Braxton barked to his younger partner. "I'll worry about Griffin."

Jordan leapt out of the car without a word. The first thing he did was run toward where Mike was lying on the ground. From the car he hadn't been able to tell whether he was alive or dead. *Please don't let him be dead. How will I ever explain to his*

122

wife? This was my call; I talked Mike into this so if he dies it's all on me, I'm the only one to blame. But now that he was closer, he could hear Mike groaning in pain as one of the detectives—Detective Andy Matthews—applied pressure to his stomach and left side. But pain was good in this situation; at least it meant he was still alive and conscious.

"Mike," Jordan said breathlessly, falling on his knees next to him. "What happened?"

"He pulled a gun on me," Mike wheezed. "That vest saved my life."

"The bullet caught him in the side," Detective Matthews said. "I think he might have bruised a few ribs, but it's nothing life-threatening. We'll look after him, you go help Rogers with crowd control before things get out of hand."

Jordan gave Mike a swift smile and a clap on the shoulder. Then he went to help the detective who was standing in front of the restaurant door. Finally, with quite a bit of yelling and waving their badges around, they managed to shepherd everyone back inside the building. Here, Jordan seized the microphone that was used for the intercom system.

"If every could please just listen to me," he said, trying to sound as calm and polite as possible. In his experience, this usually did a great deal to soothe people's nerves. In this case, however, the method had very little effect; a few people stopped talking and nudged their friends to make them do the same but most people paid him no attention.

"All right everyone, I need silence right now!" he yelled into the microphone. That made everyone stop talking. Jordan waited for the last few murmurs to die away before raising the microphone once again. This time he used a far quieter tone of voice.

"Thank you. I must ask everybody to remain inside the building until we get the parking lot cleaned up."

"And how long is that going to take?" an irritable-looking man from the back of the crowd interrupted him.

"We estimate about thirty minutes to an hour," Detective Jordan said, though that was probably a conservative estimate. Something about the man's demeanor told him to keep that thought to himself, though. "The more cooperation we have from everybody here, the sooner we will be able to get you all back to your day. But in the meantime, please return to your meals."

Gradually, the crowd dispersed, with a little encouragement from the hostess, manager and wait staff. Once Jordan was comfortable that Detective Rogers could handle the situation he went back outside, where he was pleased to see that Mike was sitting up with his back against a tree. He was still clinging to his side and trying to move as little as possible, but overall he seemed much better than he had a few minutes ago.

"Mike, I'm so sorry," Jordan said, going over to him. "I should never have subjected you to this."

"I could have said no," Mike said. "Besides, I should be thanking you. Thanks to the vest I was wearing I'm still alive."

"So no lasting harm done?"

"No. Paramedics are on the way to have a look at my ribs but I should be okay."

"Before they get here," Jordan began, pulling out his note-pad and pen, "I need to collect a statement from you. Tell me exactly what happened, with as much detail as you can, please."

"I was walking to the door of the restaurant when I heard Griffin calling me from behind," Mike began. He sounded like he had prepared what he wanted to say. "We said hello, shook hands. I asked him how he'd been lately. Then I said, 'That was probably a stupid thing to say given what you've been through the past couple days.' I was just trying to be friendly, you know? But he seemed to think it was suspicious about how I knew what he'd been through."

"And what did you tell him?"

"I lied," Mike answered. "I told him Jake called the house right after he did and told me about what happened."

"And how did he react to that?" Detective Jordan asked, his pen whizzing across the page in front of him.

"Angrily. He thought Jake had only called me for free sympathy. And he was upset that Jake hadn't bothered to call and check up on him. I couldn't think of anything to say to that so I just suggested we go inside and get out of the cold. He said yes but he seemed...distracted."

"In what way?" Jordan prompted as Mike paused.

"He kept looking anywhere but at me. Then he said he'd forgotten something and turned around like he was going to head back to his car. When he spun back around he had the gun in his hand." Mike shivered, and it had nothing to do with the cold weather.

"You heard what happened next," he finished.

Detective Jordan finished writing and stowed his notepad in his jacket before looking down at Mike with a grim smile on his face.

"You are one of the most courageous men I have ever met, Mike Levee."

Mike could think of nothing to say. Luckily, he was saved the task of coming up with something by the arrival of the ambulance. Detective Jordan stepped out of the way as the paramedics began their work. Then he looked up and saw the three detectives who had been chasing Griffin approaching the parking lot; all of them were red-faced and panting, and Detective Braxton was not with them.

"Take care of yourself, Mike; I'll check in on you later."

"Did they catch Griffin?" Mike demanded. "Was it worth it, after all of this?"

"I'm about to go find out."

He hurried over to the three men, who were now standing in a huddle on the edge of the crime scene. When they saw Detective Jordan coming toward them, one of the men spoke before he had a chance to say the first word.

"We got him. Your partner's taking him back to the station now, wants you to meet him there. Oh, and the captain wants a full report on what went down first thing when you get back."

"That's not a conversation I'll be looking forward to," Jordan muttered with a grimace on his face. He had put a civilian in harm's way and that civilian had gotten hurt. To add to that, many innocent bystanders had been put at risk. All in all he was very lucky that the situation hadn't ended up a whole lot worse.

"At least you caught the guy in the end," one of the other detectives said bracingly.

"Yeah." Then, changing the subject, Jordan asked, "Can you guys handle things here?"

They all responded in the affirmative.

"Well, considering my partner and I drove over here together it looks like I'll need to borrow somebody's car."

It was Detective Ryan who handed over his keys. Jordan slid into the driver's seat and pulled out his cell phone. He had made a promise and he planned on keeping it.

CHAPTER 19

Jake picked up the hotel room's phone on the first ring while Officer Sposito watched from the other side of the room.

"Hello?"

"It's Detective Jordan. We just took your son into custody."

Jake took a long, slow breath and let it out just as slowly.

"That's...good," he said, after a moment's hesitation. Before Griffin had actually been arrested, Jake had thought the thing he wanted most was for this to be over, for Griffin to be stopped from causing any kind of harm to anyone else. But that didn't stop some of his paternal instinct from kicking in.

"It is," Detective Jordan said with conviction. He seemed to guess at least some of what Jake was going through.

"That was a quick lunch," Jake commented, looking at his watch. It was just ten minutes past the hour. "Did everything go smoothly?"

Now it was the detective who hesitated. When he finally did speak it was clear that he was choosing his words with caution.

"Griffin decided to show his hand a bit early. Frankly, I don't think he was ever very interested in lunch."

"What do you mean he showed his hand?" Jake asked, his grip on the phone tightening; his knuckles went white and so did his face. "Did something happen to Mike?"

Officer Sposito studied Jake intently as though trying to establish some sort of mental link so he could hear what Jake was hearing.

"Mike's fine, or he will be fine," Detective Jordan said. But this was apparently not the right thing to say.

"What happened to him?" Jake was unaware that he was almost shouting; the plastic on the phone began to creak in protest because he was gripping it so tightly.

"Griffin had a gun with him, and he used it. It was before they even went inside." Jordan spoke very quickly, as though dealing out the bad news quickly would make it less unpleasant. "But we were prepared for the possibility that Griffin might come to this meeting armed, so we provided Mike with a bulletproof vest. That combined with Griffin's bad aim saved his life; the bullet might have bruised a couple of his ribs, but he'll be fine. The paramedics were just getting ready to take him to the hospital when I left."

"Thank God," said Jake. "What hospital was he going to? I'd like to go and see him."

"Actually we need you to come back down to the station," Detective Jordan said.

"Why?" Jake asked.

"I swear to you I'll explain, but I'll do it in person. Put Officer Sposito on the phone, please; I need a word with him."

"But what—"

"Now, Jake," Detective Jordan interrupted. Jake heard the bark of authority in those two simple words and knew he had no choice. He handed over the phone without another word. If Jake had hoped to pick up some kind of information about the situation from Officer Sposito's half of the conversation he was sorely disappointed. Officer Sposito's responses mainly consisted of grunting with the occasional "Yes" or "All right". He hung up after only about thirty seconds.

"So?" Jake asked impatiently. "Why am I going to the station?"

"He didn't tell me all the details," Sposito hedged. "You'll hear them from him, though."

"When?"

"As soon as you get your things together." That took Jake by surprise.

"Really?"

"Yes. We'll be on our way whenever you're ready."

Instead of trying to press for more information, Jake decided it would just be quicker and easier to obey. It only took about five minutes before they were speeding toward the police precinct. The ride over was silent. Jake appreciated the fact that the officer was giving him space to be alone with his thoughts but he wished that at least the radio was on; he didn't particularly like the thoughts that were running through his mind. Most of them were things he'd like to say to his son if given the opportunity.

Thankfully, the ride was also short. Before Jake knew it they were climbing the stairs and Officer Sposito was ushering him towards an interview room.

"You'll just be waiting in here for a few minutes," he told Jake. "Mark and Steve—sorry, I mean Detective Jordan and Detective Braxton—will be in to speak with you shortly; they're talking with Captain Huntington right now."

"OK," Jake said. "Thanks for everything."

"Don't mention it," Sposito said. Then he left, and Jake was left alone to wait for the detectives to arrive and tell him what the plan was.

CHAPTER 20

Braxton reached the door to the captain's office at almost the same moment that his partner did.

"You caught him then?" Jordan asked.

"It was a close call; I'm not as young as I used to be. How was our impromptu undercover agent?"

"The vest we gave him saved his life," Jordan said. But he felt like adding, *His life wouldn't have needed saving if I hadn't talked him into doing this.* Some of his thoughts must have shown on his face because Braxton gave him a consoling and thoughtful expression that was very unusual for him. It was a combination of concerned father and considers-himself-wise older brother.

"Ops go bad," Braxton said. "Happens to the best of us— by which I mean it's happened to me."

Jordan chuckled a little and rolled his eyes; now Braxton sounded more like himself. But then Jordan's face grew somber once more.

"Did your bad op involve a civilian?"

Before Braxton could answer the door they were both leaning against flew open. There stood their captain, looking extremely put out with both of them.

"You two have the nerve to stand outside my door talking
about bad ops but you don't have the guts to actually come
into my office and talk to me face-to-face?"

Braxton and Jordan both mumbled excuses—"It was just
an accidental meeting, sir"—"We were just about to come
in"—but Captain Huntington waved away their words and
pointed into his office. It was incredible how much they both
felt like they had just been sent to the principal's office.

When all of them were seated, Captain Huntington said,
"That was an awfully quick lunch. Detective Jordan, would you
care to explain why?"

As much as he wanted to speak to the leg of the desk, Jordan looked his captain directly in the eyes as he explained how
the situation had played out, including the statement he'd taken
from Mike Levee. Braxton filled in the details of Griffin actually being taken into custody. When they had finished their re-
telling, there was silence for a few moments. Then Captain
Huntington broke it.

"You're lucky you caught your man and that Mike Levee's
going to be alright. Otherwise I'd have no choice but to give
you a serious reprimand. Mr. Levee isn't planning to file charges is he?"

That wasn't my impression, sir," Detective Jordan replied, shaking his head. "He seemed more grateful than anything else."

"Then for now let's worry about the bigger issue facing us: getting Griffin Henderson to confess to what he's done. I'm hoping his father will be able to give us some insight we can use against him. Is he here already?"

"Yes," Detective Jordan replied.

"Bring him in here then, if you would."

Jordan left and soon returned with Jake in tow. Jordan offered Jake his seat and then everybody waited for the police captain to start speaking.

"I'm going to get straight to the point, Jake. We need your help with the interrogation of your son. This is going to be difficult for you to hear..."

"Just say it," said Jake.

"Is there any information you could give us, any sort of leverage, that would help us get Griffin to confess?"

Jake had guessed that the request was coming but he still had to think for a moment before coming up with an answer.

"If you insinuate that telling the truth would hurt me in some way, that might help you. And when he starts feeling like he's backed into a corner he'll give really snappy responses, and start drumming out a rhythm on the table or on the side of his leg. So if he does either of those things you'll know you're getting somewhere."

"Thank you, Jake," said Captain Huntington. "There's one other thing; we would like you to be in the observation room while Detectives Jordan and Braxton here conduct the interview. We need to know whether or not he's telling the truth about certain things. The plan—if you're willing to participate, that is—is for you to be in radio contact with them so you can tell them any additional information you feel is necessary."

"And my son won't be able to see or hear me?" The captain shook his head. "All right then. I'll agree to that."

"Excellent. In that case let's head down to the interview room. I'll be in observation with you, Jake; I want to watch how this one plays out."

The two detectives stopped in the observation room as well to test the radio communication, making sure they could hear Jake. Once everything was in order they went back out into the hallway and Jake heard a door open and close.

Then Detective Braxton's voice came crackling through a small circular intercom next to a window with closed blinds: "Good afternoon, Griffin."

"I beg to differ," Griffin replied sarcastically. Jake felt himself tense up when he heard that voice. At that moment, Griffin was not his son; he was just the worthless criminal that had murdered his daughter.

Captain Huntington reached out and opened the blinds and Jake was presented with a view of the back of Detective Braxton's head as he leaned against the two-way mirror. Then Braxton shifted position a little and Jake was able to see Detective

Jordan seated at a table, facing away from him. Finally, he looked past the detective to the only person in the room whose face he could actually see.

CHAPTER 21

"Good afternoon, Griffin," said Detective Braxton as he and Detective Jordan entered the room. Detective Jordan sat at the table while Braxton leaned against the mirror that doubled as the window into the observation room.

"I beg to differ," Griffin replied, holding up his shackled hands.

Remembering that there was someone actually watching, Braxton readjusted his position. Griffin raised his head, looked past Braxton into the glass and smiled. Actually it looked more like a leer, and it made Braxton's skin crawl. Did he know or somehow guess that his father was watching from behind that glass? Braxton hoped Jake would be able to retain his composure.

"Something funny, Griffin?" Detective Jordan asked politely.

"Not funny, per se," Griffin replied. "It's just that this morning didn't really end up like I expected."

"So how was it supposed to go?"

But this time Griffin didn't answer.

"I'd say it was a bit of a total failure on your part," Braxton said from his position against the wall. "You couldn't even kill that man—what was his name?"

"Mike Levee," Jordan supplied, pretending to check his notes. Braxton meanwhile was watching Griffin's face very closely.

"He's not dead?" Griffin asked. His tone suggested that he was pleasantly surprised, but his eyes gave him away; Braxton saw frustration flash through them, even though it was only there for a second. Then Griffin added, "That's…That's good."

"Is it?" said Jordan quietly. "I would have thought you'd be disappointed in your own lack of skill."

"What are you talking about?" It was Griffin's fingers that betrayed him this time; they started tapping out a rhythm against his leg.

"You're getting somewhere, he's nervous," came Jake's voice through the earpiece.

"Why did you run?" Braxton asked Griffin. "You have to admit, that looks suspicious."

"Like you wouldn't run if someone drove up beside you and pulled out a gun?" Griffin snapped. The anger; there was the other thing Jake had warned them about.

Neither detective made any response to what Griffin said.

"Well, I guess maybe you guys wouldn't," Griffin continued. "But that's because you're trained to shoot other people.

You're probably experts at shooting criminals and then making it look like an accident. We had to learn all about that sort of thing when I took my criminal justice classes."

"Where did you take these classes?" Jordan asked. "I think your professor needs to be fired."

Braxton shifted his attention away from Griffin onto his partner.

"How long have you been doing this job, Mark?"

"Coming up on 23 years now," Jordan answered. "Hard to believe it's been that long. And you've been doing it longer than I have, right?"

Braxton nodded. "I just had my 30th anniversary this past month."

"And in all that time—" Jordan began, but Griffin cut him off.

"Are you trying to scare me with how much experience you have? Because that's not going to work. All that shows me is that your skills aren't what they used to be." But was that a little sheen of sweat that Braxton saw on his forehead? He thought it was.

Jordan looked at him impassively and said, "No scare tactics here. I was just going to ask, in all the time you've been doing this, Steve, how many times have you drawn your gun?"

"Four times," Braxton answered. "But only as a way of scaring whatever suspect I was chasing. I only pulled the trigger when I was sharpening my skills on the firing range."

"I've only drawn mine three times," said Jordan. In the same breath he asked, "Why would we want to scare you, Griffin?"

"Well you obviously think I was the one who tried to kill Mike."

"Did you?" Jordan asked at the same time that Braxton said, "Not just him."

Griffin didn't know how to respond to that. He looked from one detective to the other and there was no mistaking the fear in his eyes now. His fingers even stopped their restless movement for a second, before picking up again at a faster tempo.

Braxton and Jordan shared a satisfied smile. Then Jake's voice came through their earpieces once more.

"Your captain has some information that he needs to share with you in person."

It was difficult for both of the detectives to conceal their inner thoughts but somehow they managed it.

"I think we'll leave you alone to think about things for a while, Griffin," Braxton said with a thin smile. He gestured for Jordan to precede him and they left the room.

CHAPTER 22

Almost as soon as the door to the interview room clicked shut, the door to the observation room banged open. Jake caught a brief glimpse of the hallway outside, but his view was quickly obscured by Braxton and Jordan entering the room.

"A few more minutes and we would have had him, Captain!" Braxton yelled before the door was fully closed. A couple of passing officers looked up curiously at his outburst, but then they saw who was yelling and went back to what they were doing.

"Close the door, Mark," Huntington said. "And you would do well to watch your tone, Detective Braxton." He waited until Braxton had mumbled an apology before continuing, "You'll like what I have to say. Or rather, what Tabitha has to say."

He gestured to the woman who was standing next to him: Tabitha Conners, forensics specialist. She was still relatively new at their station and always eager to prove herself. None-

141

theless, she flinched a little when Detective Braxton crossed his arms tightly over his chest and turned his demanding gaze on her.

"I have the smoking gun," she said, picking up an evidence bag from the table behind her and holding it up for the detectives' inspection.

"It's registered to Jacob Henderson, but Griffin's fingerprints are all over it."

"Where was it?" Braxton asked. "He didn't have it on him when we took him into custody."

"In an alleyway near the restaurant. He must have tossed it aside while he was running from you guys."

"This means you were right, doesn't it?" Jake asked, inserting himself into the conversation. "He stole my gun so he could try and frame me for murder?"

"It isn't quite that simple, Jake," Jordan said. "We know that he used this gun for the attempted murder of Mike Levee. But a good defense lawyer will just say that someone else broke in to your house and stole it, tossed it aside and Griffin just happened to find it and pick it up."

"That's bull crap," Jake said darkly.

"It is a bit of a stretch," Jordan agreed. "I'm just trying to make you see things from the other side's point of view. Don't get me wrong, this is the strongest evidence we have, but from the way things stand right now we still need that confession."

"What happens if you don't get that?" Jake asked. "Would he still go to jail now that you have physical evidence against him?"

"He would," Captain Huntington answered. "But only for attempted murder, since Mr. Levee's injuries—thankfully—were not fatal. With that charge, there would be significantly less prison time served and there's even a chance that he would get out." He gave Jake time to mull that over. When he said nothing, the captain went on, "But don't worry. Braxton and Jordan know what they're doing; we'll get him to talk."

He glared at the two detectives as if to say, *Or else.*

"Then let's go get ourselves a confession," Braxton said, rubbing his hands together as though he took genuine pleasure in the thought. "I'll take the lead this time," he added to his partner.

Jordan nodded, gave Jake a quick encouraging smile, and followed Braxton out of the room, taking the gun and the evidence folder with him. Jake turned to face the window as the door to the interview room burst open once again.

"Hello again, Griffin," Braxton said as he entered. Without waiting for Griffin to make any kind of reply, he continued, "What were we talking about before my partner and I stepped out?"

But it seemed that Griffin no longer trusted himself to speak after his previous slip.

"I think we were talking about who tried to kill Mike Levee, weren't we, Steve?" Detective Jordan supplied from his place leaning against the wall. He wasn't bothering to conceal the evidence bag containing Jake's gun. Quite to the contrary, he smacked it lightly against his thigh. It had the desired effect: Jordan could see Griffin's eyes widen, following each bounce the bag made.

"Ah yes, that's right. Do you know who it was, Griffin?" Braxton asked him, leaning across the table like a lion moving in for the kill.

"That's your job, sir," Griffin replied. He kept his tone polite, but he still wouldn't look at either of the detectives. Instead he addressed his own lap as he repeated, "I didn't see anything."

Detective Braxton gave an almost imperceptible nod to Detective Jordan who stepped forward and said, "You didn't see anybody holding this, for instance?"

And he tossed Jake's gun on the table with a loud bang; Griffin twitched but managed to contain any other reaction.

"I saw a gun, but I don't know what kind it was or anything."

"Are you detecting anything odd, here, Detective Jordan?" Braxton asked, turning in his seat to face his partner.

"I am, in fact," Jordan replied. "He said he didn't see anything."

"And then he said he saw a gun," Braxton continued.

"He said he saw a gun the first time, too."

"I'm betting that's the true story, then."

"So why would it change in the middle there?"

144

"I wonder..." Braxton said, letting his voice trail off and raising his eyebrows at Griffin.

Outside in the observation room, Jake watched in fascination. The back and forth between the two detectives was so quick, it would certainly cause a degree of confusion, especially in someone who was being subjected to a police interrogation. And most likely, the guiltier the suspect felt, the more effect it would have on them. Turning his attention to Griffin, Jake saw that the effect the conversation was having was very strong; his eyes bounced from one face to the other, even after they had stopped talking.

"When I said I didn't see anything," Griffin began after swallowing a few times, "I meant I didn't see anything important, like whoever was holding the gun."

"You should have made that a little clearer then, shouldn't you?" Jordan said; previously his voice had been if not warm then at least friendlier than Detective Braxton's. But now there was a definite chill to it.

"It's not my fault if you read too much into things," Griffin fired back.

Jordan chose not to reply to that, just shook his head and turned away to lean against the wall again; but now instead of leaning against the mirror-wall, he was off to Griffin's left side, much closer to the action. Jake wondered if there was some kind of strategy behind choosing that particular location. He supposed there must be; maybe they were attempting to make Griffin feel like he was boxed in, both literally and figuratively.

"Let me be honest with you about something, son," Braxton said; but his tone didn't sound very fatherly. "I think you're lying to me."

Griffin said nothing and he kept his face remarkably impassive but both Jordan and Braxton saw a bead of sweat form at the edge of his hairline and start to roll down the side of his face.

"And why would you think that, sir?"

"You know, maybe I'm wrong, maybe you're not lying," said Braxton, throwing his hands up in a gesture of defeat and letting them fall back onto the table with a smack. Griffin twitched again at the noise, more obviously this time. "Maybe you didn't see anything."

"Maybe you just saw red," Jordan put in. "That's what they say happens with killers, right?"

There it was, laid out in plain sight, an accusation as clearly tangible as Jake's gun sitting there in the middle of the table. But incredibly, Griffin still feigned ignorance.

"I don't understand what you mean, Detective Braxton."

In answer, Braxton threw his hands up in the air again, this time in an exaggerated show of frustration. He stood up very quickly from the table, which made Griffin not just twitch but actually jump.

"The game's up Griffin!" he yelled. He snatched the evidence folder out of Detective Jordan's grasp and shook it in Griffin's face. "Do you know what's in this folder? The evidence against you! Your fingerprints all over this gun, your father's gun."

"I never stole anything," Griffin denied.

Braxton paused, and the silence rang with triumph.

"We never said anything about stealing did we?" Detective Jordan asked his partner.

"No, I don't believe we did, Mark," Braxton replied. He could almost see the wheels turning in Griffin's mind as he tried to think of a way to cover up his latest slip of the tongue.

"Well…well obviously you don't think my dad shot him, or he'd be the one in this chair right now. And he would never give me anything out of the goodness of his heart—mainly because there is no goodness in his heart—so it seems logical to me that you think I stole it."

"That's a pretty lame excuse if I'm honest," said Detective Jordan after pausing for just long enough to get Griffin's heart racing.

"Filled with flaws," Braxton agreed. He collapsed back into his chair and began ticking off the flaws on his fingers. "Flaw number one: your fingerprints are also all over the inside of your father's home."

"He and I got together earlier this evening," Griffin said; there was now a faint note of desperation in his voice. "It's what people tend to do after losing a loved one."

"Flaw number two," Braxton continued, paying no heed to Griffin's interruption. "I never made a single mention of us believing your father is innocent."

"So why isn't he under arrest?"

"Flaw number three: we both know this isn't about a stolen gun."

"Don't forget flaw number four," Jordan chimed in, seating himself next to Detective Braxton. "There's one thing you forgot to deny, Griffin: you never said you didn't use that gun to try and end Michael Levee's life this morning."

Silence fell once more, spinning out longer and longer. But this time Griffin really was stuck for anything to say. Finally he sighed and leaned back in his chair. He knew that acceptance of his guilt was the only way forward.

CHAPTER 23

I should have practiced my aim a little more," Griffin said. "If Mr. Levee had just died like he was supposed to I wouldn't be having this problem."

The two detectives looked at one another in surprise. Had they really gotten their confession just like that?

"Actually you'd have an even bigger problem," said Jordan. "What I don't understand is why did you do it to begin with?"

"Get me some paper and something to write with and I'll spell it out for you."

"I'm sorry?" Braxton asked.

"Isn't that how this works? I write down my statement, you use that against me in court?"

"The thing is, that whole bit usually happens at the end of an interview," Braxton said. "That way the police can make sure the written statement matches up with what was said. But this interview is nowhere close to being over yet."

That actually did throw Griffin off his game.

"What do you mean?" he asked with a hard swallow that was just shy of being a gulp of fear.

"Well we've cleared up the matter of Mike Levee's attempted murder, but there are still four more crimes we have to discuss," Braxton said in reply. Griffin frowned but said nothing, his eyes darting from one face to the other.

"I don't have to say anything to you," he said.

"No. But you can still listen." Jordan turned his attention to his partner and asked, "Shall we work our way backwards or start from the beginning?"

"Backwards works well."

"Right then: yesterday evening, you broke into your father's house and stole his gun. You've already denied that—before we even accused you of it actually, which makes me believe that you did it."

Griffin thought for a moment. Then, much to the surprise of the two detectives, he said, "Yes. I did do that."

"Why?"

"Isn't it obvious? It was a free weapon. Much less hassle than buying one for myself, whether legal or not. Plus, I figured if it was his gun he might get blamed for it; so much the worse for him, so much the better for me."

Outside, Jake felt the heat crawl up his neck; it was even harder than he'd imagined to just sit here and listen while his son said these awful things about him. And Griffin's matter-of-fact tone: that made Jake angrier than anything else. Did he really feel no kind of remorse? And, lurking in the back of

Jake's mind, another question: *How could I have brought someone up that way?*

Meanwhile, Griffin continued: "And it wasn't exactly breaking and entering since I used my own key."

"We'll let a jury decide that," Braxton said with a grim little smile that said, *I think we both know what the verdict will be.* "Now, that's two crimes dealt with and three more to go. Shall we proceed?"

"Before we do, I just have one question to ask, sir."

"And that would be?" Braxton asked, hiding his surprise.

"How did you know it was me who broke in? I mean it could have been anybody. Or did you not know it was me and were just taking your best guess?"

To Jordan, Griffin sounded for all the world like a student who had gotten a bad grade on an assignment and was discussing his mistakes with the teacher. *How can anybody be that cool under this amount of pressure?* he wondered.

It was Braxton who answered Griffin, but he spoke carefully; he knew that if he gave away too much now, Griffin could hand off the information later to make his lawyer's job a lot easier.

"Gloves would have come in handy."

"Ah. I'll remember that for future reference." In Jordan's opinion, he sounded disappointed with himself for making such a mistake; and yet his confidence—no, arrogance, confidence was too nice of a way to put it—that he would have a future was staggering.

"Moving on to the next crime you'll be convicted of," Braxton pressed on, clearly thinking along the same lines as his partner, "another murder: Tony Mazarria, killed early yesterday afternoon."

"Oh, the drug dealer. Yeah, he had to go. Too dangerous to keep him alive."

"Care to elaborate?" Braxton prompted him. He didn't expect Griffin to actually continue, but Griffin once again defied expectations.

"He saw something he shouldn't have. The location near my father's house was just a happy accident. I didn't plan that part of it."

"But you did plan the other part of it, didn't you?" said Braxton, launching on Griffin's latest slip of the tongue.

"What other part?" Griffin asked; he hesitated only for the space of half a second, but it was enough to let both detectives that he was aware of his mistake. Braxton's heart began to beat a little faster; he knew they were getting close to the big moment, the full and ultimate confession. And there would be no break this time, no giving Griffin a chance to prepare himself.

"Your dead sister's phone was found on Tony's body," Braxton said in a quiet but dangerous voice. It was a harsh way to phrase it and he hated that Jake was there to have to hear it, but getting straight to the point definitely seemed like the best way to intimidate Griffin. "Now why would he have your sister's phone? Your sister's phone, moreover, with your fingerprints all over it?"

This was it. No more games, no more beating around the bush, no more cryptic turns of phrase. This was the moment when the truth would come out—the truth, the whole truth, and nothing but the truth. Even after thirty years as a police officer, it still gave Braxton a rush of satisfaction to finally get to this moment.

But Griffin would not give him that satisfaction.

He leaned back in his chair and said, "Pen. Paper. Now. I'm not saying another word."

It was clear that no amount of persuasion was going to change his mind, so the detectives had no choice but to leave.

CHAPTER 24

So that's it?" Jake demanded as soon as Braxton and Jordan entered the observation room. "You're not going to go back in there and take another crack at him?"

"No. We have no choice, Jake," Jordan said. "Interview's over."

"But we did get a lot of information out of him—enough to convict him of the lesser charges if not for the murder of your daughter," Braxton told him. "Your son will not be able to hurt you or anyone else for a long time."

Jake turned away from him and stared through the glass at Griffin, now hunched over a yellow legal pad, scribbling. Was he pouring out his soul, recording his reasoning behind the murder of his older sister? It was all well and good for the police department; they had closed their case and there seemed to little doubt that Griffin would be convicted and spend the foreseeable future in jail. For them it was over. But for Jake, it felt like it had only just begun.

He was burning with questions about how the whole criminal process worked. How long would a trial take? How long would Griffin spend in jail, and where would he be in the meantime? Jake knew the detectives and Captain Huntington would be able to answer all these questions, and he certainly planned on asking them. But they couldn't answer the questions weighing most heavily on his mind. Only one person could do that.

"I want to speak with my son," Jake said, turning back to face Braxton and Jordan.

"Why?" Braxton asked him.

"Because I deserve to know why he did this. What could twist somebody's mind to the point where they would want to kill their own sister?"

"I can't answer that question, Jake," Captain Huntington said. "But I understand what you're going through. It hurts to lose a child but it hurts even more to think that the child was lost due to the actions of another member of your family. You feel like you've lost two children instead of just one."

Jake gaped at him and wondered how this man was able to articulate so perfectly what he himself was going through.

"Then you know why I want to see him," Jake said, doing his best to keep his voice calm and level; he didn't want the captain to know that speaking with Griffin was more of a need than a mere desire. "Griffin's the only person who can answer my question, and I want to hear the words come out of his own mouth."

"I'm afraid I can't allow that to happen."

For a few moments, Jake said nothing at all, just glared at Huntington. Then he dropped his eyes.

"I thought you said you understood how I felt."

"I do. But letting you in the room with him now will alter his frame of mind, which in turn may alter the statement he's writing down right now."

"In other words, it will make him less likely to confess," Jordan added. "He might decide to leave something out of that written statement."

"But he'll say it to me," Jake argued. "He'll tell me why he killed Anne because he knows it will hurt me and you guys will be out here listening and you'll be able to use what he says during court, right?"

"Wrong," Braxton said. *On several levels actually,* he thought but didn't add out loud. He let his partner—the calmer one, the "good cop"—take over the explanation.

"Even if he did explain everything to you—and given the things he said about you in there just now, I'm not so sure he would—we wouldn't be able to use it because he didn't say it directly to us."

"So in order for you to use what he says against him you have to actually be in the room?" Jake asked, just to clarify.

"Or the evidence can come from the non-coerced written statement which he willingly hands over to us," Jordan replied, correctly guessing where Jake was planning on taking his argument next.

It was only with great difficulty that Jake accepted there was no possible way he was going to speak to his son right now. He would just have to wait. And he was prepared to wait all day if it came to it.

"Can I wait here until he's finished?"

Jake looked up in time to see all three men exchanging puzzled looks.

"I'm afraid I don't understand you, Jake," Captain Huntington said with a frown. Jake also frowned, but his was an expression of frustration rather than confusion. These men were detectives, why did they seem so incapable of grasping the obvious?

"Can I wait here until he finishes his statement? Because after he's done with that I can speak to him without altering his mental state, or whatever you said."

"Oh. I see," Captain Huntington said. He sighed and continued, "You won't be able to speak to him then, either. In fact, you will not be able to speak to him until the trial begins. And if I'm being honest with you, that process usually takes quite a while to complete."

Something took over in Jake's mind when he heard those words. He didn't know if it was the emotions that had been building up for days with no outlet, or some kind of paternal instinct. Most likely, it was a combination of the two. But all Jake knew was that he was powerless to try and fight it. So he gave in willingly, relishing the freedom it provided from having to try and think rationally.

"That's my son in that room. I have every right to see him and you can't stop me!" Jake yelled.

He made a move as though to stride out the door and Braxton, Jordan and Huntington all moved in unison, almost as though this was a fully rehearsed, choreographed routine. Before Jake could process what was happening, Jordan and Huntington were blocking the door and Detective Braxton had pinned Jake's arms behind his back.

"Let me go," Jake growled, struggling fruitlessly to break free.

"Not until you've calmed down," Braxton said, tightening his grip even more.

"Do you really want to talk to Griffin like this?" Jordan asked. Although adrenaline was running through him, he somehow managed to keep his voice low, rational, calm. "Would you even listen to anything he had to say in this state?"

Jake still looked furious, but Braxton felt his resistance ebb ever so slightly. Behind Jake's back, he nodded at his partner to keep talking. As for Captain Huntington, he knew better than to interrupt. Detective Jordan's gift for being able to diffuse situation was truly a rare talent and they certainly had need of it in this situation.

"Listen to me, Jake." Jordan took one small step away from the door, his hand held out in from of him not as a shield but as a gesture of peace. "You're exhausted, and I don't blame you. Actually I think you've held yourself together remarkably well give what you've been through in the past couple of days." He took another step closer. "What you need right now is some peace and quiet, a chance for you to clear your head, to start thinking straight—"

But he had finally said the wrong thing.

"Don't you understand?" Jake roared. He came very close to getting away from Braxton, who had let his grip slacken. In that moment, if only subconsciously, Jake understood what it meant to be angry enough to kill. I would be such a relief to take some of the pain that he was feeling and transfer it to someone else.

"Don't you get it?" he repeated. "I'll never be able to think straight about this. No one ever could."

"Would knowing why really help you to be able to cope, Jake?" Jordan asked, recovering his composure very quickly following the rapid shift in the tone of the situation. His left hand was still held out in front of him but his right was now edging toward the holster on his hip.

"Yes, it would."

"But how? Just tell me how it would help you, really think about it."

Jake actually did slow down for a moment as his rationality made a brief attempt to reassert itself.

"I don't know," he admitted.

"Exactly," Jordan agreed, pleased that he was having the desired effect. "And until you can answer that question you need to walk away from this."

Again, Braxton felt Jake's resistance begin to lessen, but he did not loosen his grip this time.

"How can I walk away?" Jake asked, and now tears began to run slowly down his cheeks. Jordan thought they had finally reached the heart of the matter, the real reason that Jake was fighting them so hard. The next thing Jake said confirmed his theory.

"My son killed my daughter. I have no one left."

So that was the real reason Jake wanted to see his son so badly. He was afraid of the unknown, so he was reaching out to connect with the only thing in this situation that was familiar. It just so happened that the person he was reaching out to was the one who had caused the unfamiliar situation to begin with.

"There are other people who can help you," Jake," said Jordan. "I will, for one. And so will my partner, and my captain. We'll talk things over with you as much as you want, answer whatever questions you have. You don't have to go through this alone."

"He's right, Jake," Braxton said. All he could see of Jake was his trembling back and shoulders, but he knew things were moving in the right direction now. "There are others besides you who have been through something like this. We can put you in touch with them, find support groups for you to join. I know it's hard for you to hear but reaching out to Griffin will not help you. It's only going to make it hurt worse, like rubbing salt in the wound."

Jake knew he was right. Every time he looked at his son now or even thought about him, it would be a reminder of this whole terrible ordeal. For once, Jake had to put his own needs before the needs of others, even if that meant turning his back on his own flesh and blood. Maybe forgiveness would come later. But in order for that to happen, he had to give himself time to heal.

It took a concentrated effort, but Jake made himself stand perfectly still, letting all the tension in his muscles drain away. After about a minute or so, Braxton deemed it safe to let him go. Jake wiped his face with the back of his hand. He knew he should apologize for his behavior, but he also knew that the words "I'm sorry" wouldn't even begin to cover it.

"Why don't I give you a ride home?" Detective Jordan offered.

"Sure," Jake said, or tried to say; it came out as a barely audible croak. He cleared his throat and tried again. "Sure. I'd appreciate that, thank you."

And after saying goodbye to Braxton and Huntington, he followed Detective Jordan out of the room without once looking through the observation window.

On the other side of the glass, Griffin continued to write.

CHAPTER 25

It took him almost an hour to finish; when he finally did, there were many edits and crossing-outs. At the end of it, Griffin shuffled the pages together and leaned back in his chair to look over what he had written one last time.

My name is Griffin James Henderson. I am a thief and a murderer. To be more precise, I've killed two people in as many days, and almost killed another. I only really planned on committing two murders: the first victim (my sister) and the one that failed (my father's friend Mike Levee). But things didn't quite go as I'd intended; they never do, do they? Anyway, that led to the necessity of killing my second victim. Although he really wasn't much of a loss, was he? Tony Mazarria, I mean. The way I see it, I did the police a favor by killing him.

But I'll come back to that in a minute. I need to start from the beginning.

Technically this all started when I was fifteen and my mother died in a car accident. Our family basically fell apart after that happened. My sister was there for me for a while, but then she turned eighteen. She'd had enough of living in that house, with my worthless father too drunk or too high to bother with raising two teenagers.

I didn't blame Anne for wanting to leave, but I was angry that she didn't take me with her. While she was out living her own life, I still had another year and a half to stay at home with my dear old dad. To make things worse, all of Mom's stuff was still lying around because he was too scared to face moving it. I guess maybe he was trying to pretend that she could still come back.

Don't worry, I won't bore you with every detail of my life from the age of sixteen to the present day; most of it I don't remember anyway, or don't care to. I'll just say that the next year or so was pretty rough. My dad did end up getting help for his drug habit, but he still wasn't there for me; now he was too busy with meetings and withdrawal. And who was left to deal with him when he failed, when he started to relapse? Not his sponsor. His sponsor got to go home to his family and live his perfect little life.

But not me. There was no escape from it for me. For the last six months that I lived with my father, I started using the stuff he was trying to give up. I knew who to get it from since he wasn't exactly sneaky about going out to stock up when his supply ran low. It was the only way I could cope; otherwise I think I would have stolen his gun and killed myself.

I thought everything would get better after I moved out, but I was wrong. I couldn't find a job so I ended up moving in with Anne for a little while. But it was awful; I was on edge constantly, worried that she would find out about my little habit that was fast becoming an addiction. And I was still angry with her. She was moving on with her life, had a good job and friends and a dream she could chase. It was like she didn't even miss Mom any more.

Fast forward a few years. I had finally managed to kick my drug habit. I took an occasional hit now and then when things got rough, but the problem was nowhere near as bad as it had been. Now I was living on my own and had work to keep me busy, but I was still hurting inside. So I added another distraction onto my plate: taking classes in criminal justice.

I honestly believe that was one of the best choices I've ever made. A lot of the stuff we studied involved the motives behind the crimes of different killers, real-life murderers. It was then that I realized how much I had in common with a lot of them. The crappy childhood had a lot to do with it, and the built-up anger.

At least most of my anger was now focused purely on my father. He had a choice about whether or not to abandon me; he chose wrong. As a result I was left feeling like I'd lost both my parents instead of just one. It was then that I decided to use my newly obtained knowledge to cause my father as much pain as possible. I thought I would be able to do it without getting caught. But I guess I wouldn't be writing this if that was the way things had turned out.

One thing I will say to my father's credit: when he was actually himself, he was a very caring person, always putting other people first. And that was the weakness I would exploit. Killing him outright would be too kind. Why let him die when I could make him live with a lifetime of pain by killing everyone he loved?

Of course, I knew I would have to somehow insert myself into the investigation to be able to watch him suffer. How was I to do that without attracting suspicion from the cops? I had to make them come to me. Therefore, the victim had to be someone I was closely associated with, someone who my father also cared about. Anne was the perfect fit.

It took a while to plan everything out; I knew I had to consider every last detail so the crime wouldn't be traced back to me. When I was ready, I made the phone call inviting Anne to dinner. She accepted, said she couldn't wait.

We met outside Jack's Fishery at 6:30 pm on Friday, the 12th of December. I waited until we were almost finished eating to suggest that we go buy some flowers for our mother's grave; it was ten years since she died. Anne thought it was a sweet idea.

"But where are we going to find flowers at this time of night?" she asked; because it was nearly 8:00 by this point.

"I go to school with one of the guys who works down at the florist's shop," I told her. This was a total lie but she had no way of knowing that. "I'll give him a call."

And I stepped away from the table and went outside to pretend to make the call. When I had been gone for a reasonable length of time I went back inside.

"Well?" she asked me.

"He'll let us in the back door. His boss would be angry if he let someone through the front after hours."

The florist shop that I was talking about, as I'm sure you smart detectives have figured out by now, was the shop that her body was found behind. When we got there I let her go first down the alleyway toward the back door. The last thing she did in this life was laugh, saying she felt like a criminal for doing this.

But I was the criminal. I picked up the loose brick I had planted there earlier that day and smashed her in the back of the head with it, over and over again until I was sure that she was dead. Then I put down the brick and carried her body to the lit-up back parking lot.

Remember, my main goal was to cause my father as much pain as possible, so I wasn't interested in hiding my work. That's why I was careful with her face, too; I wanted her to be easily identified. For good measure, I left her wallet. But I took her phone; it wouldn't do for the police to find that and discover the text messages she'd sent me firming up the details of our dinner plans.

Once the crime scene was arranged I took the roses I'd bought earlier that day and put them on my mother's grave. I guess my father must have moved on, too because there was no sign that he had been there. So far I thought everything had gone off without a hitch. I decided to go grab a little cocaine to celebrate. I usually got it from Tony but when he saw me he backed away real quick. I asked him what was wrong.

All he said was, "Been to any flower shops lately?"

I almost killed him right then; looking back, that's what I should have done. But I just settled for threatening him and hoped that would be enough until I could plan things out so I could kill him without getting caught.

The next day the police came to my work and asked me to come down to the station with them. You know all that bit. Only when I said I was going to take a walk to the bus stop I was actually going to tail Tony. I watched from around the corner while he and my dad argued with each other. Then he headed straight for me. I tightened my grip on the big chuck of cinderblock I had found.

Tony was dead before he knew what was happening. I took the concrete block with me; it's now floating at the bottom of the river along with the brick I used to kill Anne and the shoes that Tony spilled his blood on. Anne's cell phone should be there, too; that was a mistake on my part, leaving it with Tony's body. I had wiped all the data, but I thought the investigation would be more likely to turn to my father if something tied Tony to Anne. So I put her phone in his pocket, then scooped up his supply and went home.

Later that day, my phone rang; it was the police again, asking me to come back to the precinct because they had a few more questions for me. I have to admit, I was terrified. Did they somehow know it was me who killed Tony? If they figured that out, then it would be an easy jump to conclude I had killed Anne, too. Yeah, looking back on it, leaving the phone there was a really stupid move.

But they didn't even ask about Tony; all they wanted to know was stuff about Karl. I gave them some more fake information and they said I could go. But just as I was walking out, Detective Braxton asked if I knew who Tony was. I said I didn't, but I don't think he believed me. I was afraid I was going to get arrested right then. Obviously I didn't, but now I knew they were on to me. What could I do to fix that?

I decided the best course of action would be to turn the attention off of me and onto someone or something else. Another crime had to be committed. Mike Levee had almost been my primary victim before I settled on Anne; my father would know about his death, but as far as I knew the police had no idea that I had any sort of contact with him. Now that worked in my favor because I would be safe from suspicion. To make sure my father was the main suspect, I also decided to use his gun to commit the crime; it's exactly the kind of stupid thing he would do if he were ever to actually murder someone.

Hence, the necessity of breaking into his house and stealing it. I was glad I had kept my old key; picking the lock or breaking a window or something would have left too much evidence. I did wear gloves, but they were too bulky; I had to take them off in order to enter the safe combination and make sure the gun was loaded.

It was only after I was on my way home that I realized what a terrible mistake I had made. Not just with taking the gloves off but with using my own key. As far as I knew, the only people who had a key to my father's house were himself, my sister, and me. Since one of those was already dead and the other one lived in the house, I had just drawn a lot more attention onto myself.

That's the problem with impulsive crimes; you make mistakes. Anne's murder was good—very little forensic evidence. But with all the crimes that came after I made stupid mistakes.

I asked myself, where was the first place the detectives would look, given that they were already on to me? The obvious answer was my apartment. At least now I had a ready-made excuse to start fresh, get away from this town I'd lived in my whole life.

But in the meantime I needed a place to lay low. Mike's son would be a good person to stay with; he would be sure to back up whatever alibi story I came up with. I called Mike to set up our lunch meeting, and he told me that Alex was out of town. Even better. I spent the night at Alex's house and went the next morning to meet Mike.

I imagine he'll tell you everything I said and did from that point on. I won't bore you by writing it down again. But before my story comes to an end, I'll just say one more thing: make sure my father reads this, or at least hears about it at my trial. Yes, I know I'm going to trial and it's a trial I will probably lose; my defense lawyer is probably going to hate my guts for writing down all this information for the prosecution to use.

But I really don't care if I end up in jail. If anything, that will cause my father even more heartache, knowing that he's responsible not only for his daughter's death but also for the incarceration of his son.

My father made me who and what I am.

You make sure he knows that.

CHAPTER 26

Jake drove up to the place on the hill where his wife and daughter were buried. He got out of the passenger's side with one bouquet of flowers and Mike Levee got out of the driver's side with another bouquet.

Jake took the flowers that Mike was holding and knelt in front of the tombstones. While Mike looked on, Jake brushed the snow from the engraved granite so he could see the writing. They had both died on the same day, exactly ten years apart.

Fifteen years since Margie had died, five years since he lost Anne. And four since Griffin had gone to prison. He would stay there for the rest of his life. Jake wrote to him in jail at least once a week. He figured extending the olive branch was the best thing he could do to make some good out of a bad situation. In all the time Jake had been writing he had only ever received one response, consisting of two words:

"No way."

That had been Griffin's answer when Jake made the suggestion about being buried on this hilltop with the rest of the Henderson family. He would be the only one missing; Jake's name and date of birth were already etched into the granite next to his wife's.

Jake thought about how much his life had changed over the past five years. So much loss, yes, but he had gained things, too: friends from the counseling sessions he'd attended, and a new confidence in his own ability to deal with loss.

Now he was starting fresh, leaving all of this behind him. Mike was driving him to the airport so he could fly down the east coast to Florida; he thought the warmth would do him good. But even while he was down there, Jake still planned to keep writing to his son, keep trying to convince him about being buried with the rest of his loved ones. Griffin wanted to excuse himself from the family that—in his mind, at least—had caused him so much pain. But Jake wouldn't let him do that. After all, family was family and blood was the strongest bond of all.

ABOUT THE AUTHOR

Emily Davidson is a young writer currently living in Virginia. She studied Creative Writing at Longwood University, where she graduated in 2013. When she's not writing, Emily enjoys reading, spending time with her family and her dog, and relaxing with friends. This is her first novel.